Shoppi

and Other Stories

Suzanne Greenberg

© 2024 Suzanne Greenberg

All rights reserved for the author.
Please contact the author for permissions.

Logo by Morgan G Robles

Arroyo Seco Press

www.arroyosecopress.org

Cover art: hxdbzxy from iStock

ISBN: 979-8-9895659-4-8

For Steve, who makes me laugh and knows how to cry

Contents

Under the Radar 1
How It Happens 5
Missing 11
Remodel 18
Night Shift 26
Viola 36
Come See Us Again 45
Offering 53
Shopping for Dad 60
Juggling 63
Freshman 68
How This Works 75
Illegal Baker 81
Stampede 88
Show Me Something 98
Not for You 102
Afterword iii
Acknowledgements v
Biography vii

Under the Radar

It was hard for me to pretend it was fun riding around on the back of a golf cart. Guy liked to fly under the radar. That's what my mother said whenever I complained about it.

"What's flying got to do with it?" I asked.

"It's an expression," my mother said. "A figure of speech."

We were washing the dog in the backyard and up to our elbows in soap bubbles. Last summer, before he left us, I used to look out the kitchen window and see my father soaping up the dog, talking to him all the while. You're a good dog, he'd say. What a dog. But my mother didn't talk to Ernie. She washed him the same way she scrubbed the shampoo through my hair when I came home from a day at the beach. It didn't exactly hurt, but it didn't feel good either, her fingernails so close to my scalp.

"It's not even legal," I said, "riding around on a golf cart."

"It might be," my mother said. "Guy likes to keep them guessing. The police don't know whether they should ticket him or not. Haven't you seen how they look at him?"

I'd seen. Where else was I going to look? I was always the one stuck in the backseat facing them when the police edged up behind us, elbowing each other and laughing. I'd put my hand under my shirt like I had an itch and give them the invisible finger.

"He's a clever man," my mother said, turning the hose on Ernie now, full force and cold.

I was twelve and no one would hire me for a real job, so I was stuck babysitting every afternoon at the mail-order bride's house. Mrs. Gallop spoke Russian to Nikki before she left for the gym. The words sounded thorny, like Nikki was in big trouble, but Mrs. Gallop always gave me her same quick smile before she left, so I knew it was just the way her language sounded in my ears. *Mail-order bride,* my mother said every time I went over there to babysit. *Why not just call it prostitution and be done with it?*

"Be a good girl for Sally," Mrs. Gallop said.

"Don't worry about us," I said. I listened to my words extra hard when I spoke to Mrs. Gallop, wondering how I sounded to her.

Sometimes Mrs. Gallop flipped on the music she worked out to before she even left the house, and I could hear the Russians singing loud in her tiny headphones. She hated the United States and California in particular. *It's unnatural to have this much sunshine,* she told me once with her accent. Even on a cloudy day, Mrs. Gallop made a little visor above her eyes with the side of her hand when she walked outside.

I thought she could benefit from sunglasses, but Mrs. Gallop always put big, gray earmuffs over her headphones and headed out the door. *Like she's still in Russia,* my mother said. *Like she might be headed off on her dog sled.*

"Play treasure hunt," Nikki said as soon as her mother shut the door. "Close your eyes."

I shut my eyes while Nikki hid toys. Sometimes I'd cheat and peek, but it didn't really matter since Nikki always hid them in the same spots — under the kitchen sink, under her small bed, and under her mother and father's bigger one. I got sick of this game before we even hit July. Still, it kept Nikki happy, and I was too lazy to come up with something better.

"Let's see," I said when she was done hiding everything. "Where should I start?" I looked under the couch pillows in the living room, and then I went into the kitchen and looked in the refrigerator because I was hungry. I opened the vegetable bin and the cheese bin. The food in this house looked nothing like our food. The vegetables were twisted-looking roots, and the cheese was wrapped in white paper. When Nikki wanted a snack, I'd dig around until I found something I recognized, like an orange.

"You're not really looking," Nikki said, behind me now.

I reached in my pockets and pulled out one of the gummy bears I always brought with me for bribes. "Open wide," I told Nikki. Then I popped one in her mouth.

I heard the metallic-sounding horn of Guy's golf cart, and Nikki and I went to the living room window and looked out. Guy was at the wheel and my mom was riding shotgun and waving big like she was a beauty pageant contestant sitting in a convertible. "Come on out here, girls!" she said. "We're going for a ride."

I had never left the house with Nikki before when I was babysitting, but I figured it would be all right as long as we got back before Mrs. Gallop did.

"This is cool," Nikki said when I lifted her onto the backseat of the golf cart.

"Who wants to go for ice cream?" Guy said, taking off before we could answer.

"Where's the seatbelt?" Nikki asked. "Do I need a helmet?"

"It's okay," I told her. "We're flying under the radar."

At Rite Aid, I held Nikki up, so she could study her ice cream choices. I could hear my mom and Guy kissing behind us, and I hoped that no one I knew was going to walk in. *Be happy your mother's finally happy*, my mom said when I made a face at her one morning while Guy was singing in our shower. *Be happy someone's still interested in the old nag.*

"Rainbow sherbet," Nikki said. "On a pointy cone."

Even though I wasn't that hungry anymore, I ordered a double rocky road because I wanted to see if my mother would change my order to a single scoop the way she would have before Guy came along. But my mother was studying the ice cream choices like she'd never seen them before and whispering something to Guy that made him laugh.

"Strawberry cheesecake," my mother said. "In a cup. Two spoons."

We had parked in a regular space in front of the store, and when Nikki and I sat in the back, I reached my feet out and touched the headlights of the car behind us with my toe. We drove down the street, past the gym where Mrs. Gallop worked out. I put my arm around Nikki to hide her from the big glass window everyone faced while they exercised.

When Nikki's sherbet fell off, it landed on the street in such a perfect ball that for a minute I thought about jumping off and picking it up, sticking it right back on her cone. But instead I watched the car behind us flatten it with its tire before turning the corner. I stared at the curved rainbow left behind on the street. I had never seen Nikki cry before, and she did it so quietly, at first I didn't even notice.

"Take mine," I said.

But Nikki shook her head. "I don't like brown ice cream," she said.

Guy kept driving, his hairy elbow leaning out his window, my mother feeding him spoonfuls of strawberry cheesecake.

"You didn't even look under the beds," she said. "You have to finish the game when we get home."

A cop came around the corner and Guy beeped his tinny horn and waved. *DUI*, I'd heard my mother tell her sister on the phone. *It could be worse. At least he's not taking me out on the handlebars of his bike.*

"Scenic route time, girls," Guy said, turning by the marina, away from our neighborhood.

"I want to go home now," Nikki said.

I thought about Nikki's mother, the mail-order bride, getting home from the gym, taking off her earmuffs and then her headphones, and the way a house feels when someone's missing from it. I reached in my pocket and took out two gummy bears, one for me and one for Nikki.

"Enjoy the scenery," I said to Nikki, feeling like I was forty years old. "You'll be home before you know it."

How It Happens

Angelica is standing on top of Black Rock afraid to jump. One of her feet is planted into the wet blue towel that someone has left on the part of the rock that is the jump pad. The towel was left so long ago it's melded into the rock. The people behind her are mostly teenagers, and next to her is a middle-aged man who is talking to her the way her therapist sometimes does on Zoom. "It's okay. You've got this."

She'd like to push him, imagines him falling backwards off the side of the rock, the part you aren't supposed to jump off of. But instead she lets him grip her arm while she tries to get her left foot to move closer to her right, closer to the edge.

"I've got you," the man says.

There's a paper mask hanging off the side of the rock. The part that loops around your ear is looped around a ridge. When Angelica looks just beyond her right foot, past her toes that grip through the towel, she sees the paper mask. When she looks down, Angelica sees heads bobbing, their snorkels pointed up out of the water. Her brother, who jumped straight away, is probably one of the swimmers staring through goggles at sea turtles bigger than car engines.

Angelica knows something about car engines. Before Covid, she walked home from middle school with a boy who had a car up on risers in his family's driveway. His father said it was his if the boy could get it running by the time he got his driver's license in two years. The boy opened the hood and discussed each part with Angelica, his face as serious as the surgeon's who took out Angelica's tonsils when she was ten. When he was done explaining, they went inside and she let the boy feel her up in the kitchen while they drank the filmy chocolate almond milk his mom bought straight out of the carton.

"We're going to have the time of our lives," her mother had said. "Imagine, Hawaii."

"What lucky kids," her stepfather said. "They don't know how good they've got it."

Angelica is glad that at least her stepfather isn't standing up here next to her, his eyebrow raised in disappointment. It's bad enough that he and her mother have an adjoining room in the hotel, where she can hear them through the cracks in the door, her mother's muffled laughter and her stepfather's dull grunts that make Angelica turn up the television so loud her little brother glares at her from under his headphones attached to his computer screen.

The four of them have been at home together a year, and up here on this rock Angelica is relieved finally to be away from all of them, her stepfather pacing outside, talking on his phone too loudly in the middle of their dead-end street, her mother at the kitchen table taken over with her work folders, her hair up in Angelica's butterfly clips on days she has to be on camera. Angelica's even tired of her little brother, whose voice has leaked through their shared bedroom walls for months as he's played Minecraft online, quickly figuring out that his teachers were too overwhelmed to care as long as he turned off his camera and muted himself during Zoom classes.

But now the pandemic is over, or ending, Angelica isn't really sure. She just knows that after they swabbed the inside of their noses and the test results came back negative, they were allowed to get on a plane, and when they get back home from this vacation she and her brother might go back to school part time.

"I paid for the pre-boarding, so we could all sit together," Angelica's mother said, but Angelica would have rather sat in a different section of the plane instead of behind her stepfather, who reclined his seat all the way back as soon as the captain told them it was safe. She wished she were younger so she could kick the seatback, but she was fourteen, way too old for that.

At fourteen, she's way too old to be frozen up here on Black Rock. In the water below, sea turtles are as common as boogie boards. Still, everyone in the water clusters around each time one swims by like they've spotted a celebrity. The sea turtles make Angelica feel like her stomach is rising up to her throat the same way the chocolate almond milk did, or maybe it was the spongy pads of the boy's fingers feeling under her shirt, reaching down into her bra. If she jumps, she may land on a sea turtle. She imagines the feel of a turtle's back against her bare feet, of the crack she'll cause with her heavy landing and how her feet will break through the shell and sink straight into the turtle's slimy flesh.

"Just jump already!" someone behind her shouts.

And then that person is shushed. "Don't be a dick, dickhead. Give her time."

The man holding onto her arm says, "You got this."

Angelica wants to tell him to shut up, that he's not helping, that he can let go now. But maybe he's the only thing keeping her from falling forward, from slipping and tumbling headfirst into the water churning below.

They're all waiting. She feels their impatience bubbling, even the ones that shushed the boy who told her to jump already. He just said what they were all thinking. She knows she's become the lady in line at Ralphs with the coupons she pulls out and begins to sort through after her groceries have already been scanned. That she's the man in the return line at Costco bringing back a sixty-inch television after the Super Bowl is over, who's making everyone wait while he argues for his refund.

Angelica's wearing a bikini with cheeky bottoms, which just means her butt is hanging out, and she wishes she were wearing a one-piece. She imagined lounging by a pool in this bathing suit when she ordered it online, her mother too distracted to say no, maybe walking over to a beach bar and ordering a lemonade that would be served in a special souvenir cup shaped like a pineapple or a coconut, but instead she followed her twelve-year-old brother up to the top of Black Rock, and then he jumped and she didn't.

It's two in the afternoon in April, and the sun is out now after a rain shower. The weather is never like this in California. When it rains in California where Angelica lives, it rains for a whole day or usually more, but here it sometimes only rains for minutes. In California, the ocean is murkier, and Angelica can't see what's swimming around her. In California, she can pretend she's in the Dead Sea, which she learned in geography class is too salty to support life.

Angelica has stood in this spot on the launch pad of Black Rock through a rain shower, and now she is standing here with the sun beating down on her scalp. Angelica can feel the sun burning a red stripe down her middle part. The man gripping tight to her upper arm is probably leaving a bruise. She wants to flick off his hand as if it's a mosquito, but if she does, she might slip. The blue towel she has one foot planted on is melded into the platform of the rock, and she stares down at her right foot, her toes with the chipped blue nail polish, a different blue than the towel, and another kind of blue, a blue vein running up the middle of her foot.

Angelica got a therapist when she turned thirteen the way some of her friends got their ears pierced or had a bat mitzvah. "Because it's hard being a teenager," her mother said. "I wish someone had paid that kind of attention to me." And then the lockdown happened, and instead of sitting in a chair in his office she sat in her own chair in her room and stared at him on her computer.

"Sometimes you just need someone to talk to," her mother said. *Why can't I just talk to you,* Angelica thought but didn't say. "What if I don't have anything to say?" she asked.

"I want you to be heard," her mother said, walking away.

In person, Angelica used to notice things like a stray gray hair growing out of a place on her therapist's cheek where he had missed a spot with his razor, but on Zoom she can only tell if he didn't bother shaving at all. Once, when Angelica stared at her therapist on Zoom, she noticed he had buttoned his shirt wrong and the collar was higher on one side. Another time, she saw he'd moved a picture on the bookshelf, and she wondered where the one of his wife went, and if the dog was a new dog or if it was just a new picture.

Angelica usually wishes her life were more interesting while she waits for her therapist to ask her a question. She knows she disappoints him by not having anxiety over the pandemic. "I'm just bored," she tells him, and watches his face fall. She would like to Zoom with her therapist right now, tell him how it feels to be up here. "You're very brave," he would say.

"Let's do it together. How would that be?" the man gripping her arm next to her says. Angelica has fantasized about jumping out of an airplane with a boy she loves. Not the boy with the car who pushed his hands down into her bra, another boy with broader shoulders and maybe blond stubble on his face. In her fantasy, they are both eighteen, so they don't have to ask anyone's permission. Their parachutes open together, and they hold hands and float over towns where church bells ring, and maybe over tulip fields.

"Dude, that's a terrible idea," she hears a boy behind her say. "If she doesn't jump with you, you'll both get fucked up."

"I think I know what I'm doing," the man says.

"It's your funeral, dude," the boy says.

Angelica is afraid to back up almost as much as she's afraid to jump. She imagines slipping as she steps back, sliding off of Black Rock. She imagines the crowd of teenagers pushing her forward, *just jump, just jump.*

"Here we go," the man says. He has let go of her arm and is reaching for her hand. "You've got this."

His palm is wet from sweat or heat. Maybe he's afraid, too. She shakes free of it and steps forward, moving her left foot so it's parallel to her right.

"Just don't look down," he says.

Angelica looks up instead, lets the sun temporarily blind her, and then she is stepping off and she is on her way down. *This is what it feels like,* she thinks as she feels her body heavy and light, floating and falling. *This is how it happens.*

Missing

Mostly it's bicycles that are stolen from their tree-lined neighborhood that borders a much bleaker area. Once it was a laptop left on a dining room table, a front door unlocked for the length of time it took a neighbor to walk his corgi around the block. Once it was a bag of groceries left briefly in the open trunk of a car. It's all there on the neighborhood listserv, the husband says. Every single thing.

"They must have been hungry," the wife says, "to steal groceries." The wife has been living on a diet of chewed fingernails and gummy bears.

The husband and wife have a child who died.

No. This is a lie.

The child was born and lived and had birthday parties in the park with the pirate ship, where there was once a piñata in the shape of Dora the Explorer. There was once a party with a cake made out of five thin layers, each covered with a different pastel color of dyed vanilla icing because the child saw this cake in a book they read to her at night and wanted only this same cake or no cake at all.

And there was once a party where a mother showed up at pick-up time drunk and stoned on painkillers and wove around the park in her high heels like a wasted fairy princess before falling asleep in the sand under the slide.

"Have you ever," everyone said. "Her poor children. What a shame."

And of course there were art camps and Irish dancing classes and volunteer opportunities and short bouts of indulged vegetarianism and formal school dances with limousines and pictures by someone's backyard pool and family vacations where there were sometimes cousins and sometimes a lake and sometimes an ocean and sometimes a mountain and once a cathedral.

Mostly the mother checks out neighborhood churches online. That way she can stay in her pajamas on the couch with her laptop glowing and her cat curled up next to her. Her husband is very busy at night. He is in the home office late, scrolling online too. He is also looking for religion, but his is a religion of reason. "Who steals an old man's walker from his front porch?" he asks his wife over coffee in the morning after a night so late he may not yet have gone to sleep. "Who steals a pair of size thirteen flip-flops?"

Her mother, the girl's grandmother, is planning an anniversary party for the husband and wife. There will be martinis with olives she has already ordered from a special catalog. The olives have pits and come from Spain and are packed in jars too beautiful to recycle. They must be made into vases for the tiniest bunches of deeply trimmed irises. They must be filled with waxy oil and wicks and turned into candles. They must be filled with chocolate-dusted almonds and given out as housewarming presents. There is no end to the way these jars are to be cherished.

Even the pits of these olives are special. They will float in the waxy oil of the candles. They will be planted in the jars and sung to in Spanish.

There is one church a town over where the sermons are published online. Every week the sermons are about forgiveness. The mother is not sure if she is supposed to forgive or be forgiven. Or maybe both. Yes, probably that's it.

Their child came home from college her junior year for spring break, shut the door to her bedroom with the attached bathroom and didn't come out.

"What's happening in there? Are you okay?" the mother asked her daughter and heard nothing. "I'm coming in," the mother said, but the door was locked.

"Your father," the mother said. "He knows how to open it. Please," the mother said. "Just say something."

"I'm fine," the daughter said. "Go away."

"Can I come in?" the mother said. "I'm here if you want to talk some more."

But the daughter did not want to talk anymore. She was dumped by a boy in college. This was all she said. "Leave me alone," she said.

After bringing her daughter meals on a tray for three days, the mother had said it was time to get up and come downstairs for breakfast, and this was what happened. The lock clicked shut.

In the shower, the mother was thinking about taking her daughter to lunch, and then maybe they'd go shopping. Her daughter used to talk in the car when she was in high school. It was easier for them both to say a boy's name when they didn't have to look at each other.

After her shower, the mother knocked at the daughter's bedroom door. She planned to say, "Mexican or Japanese. You pick." The mother slowly opened the door that was no longer locked. Her daughter's suitcase was gone, her sheets and blanket pulled as tightly as compression socks across her bed.

"She's young," the husband said. "Give her time."

"It's because I pushed," the mother said. "I should have left her alone."

But the mother keeps pushing. She cannot help herself. She leaves phone messages and sends letters and emails and texts. She hears nothing. At night, she pretends to sleep, lying next to the spot where her husband is not. She has been too strict with their daughter. She has not been strict enough. She stays awake adding up the math of her mistakes.

A single cherimoya has been stolen from a neighborhood fruit tree. The tree produced nothing but plain, thick leaves for three years. And then finally this single piece of fruit. They had all been watching it grow, the whole neighborhood, wondering about the custard-like filling inside the ugly green flesh of it. And now it's gone.

One day a letter arrives for the mother addressed in her daughter's neat handwriting, and the mother leaves it on the dining room table and paces around the house for several minutes before opening it. The envelope feels explosive.

Inside there is a piece of paper, a sticky note, with the words LEAVE ME ALONE written on it in all capital letters. The mother feels like her stomach is being pulled out of her body. She sits down on the floor, and the cat curls up on her lap and purrs.

"They stole a child's scooter right out of his backyard," the husband says one morning. "Jesus," her husband says. "Enough is enough."

There is talk online about cameras. There is talk about hiring security to patrol the neighborhood in their sedans with the logos emblazoned across both sides. "The cops won't do anything," the husband says, splitting open another packet of sweetener into his coffee.

The mother finally gets in her car and drives to the church one town over. She circles the block and then parks and gets out and peers in a window. It is midweek, midday, and the church is empty, but she can see inside. There are rows of folding chairs instead of pews. The mother read online that the church is nondenominational.

She takes herself out to lunch at a restaurant nearby that serves onion soup with a thick skin of cheese over it and pokes holes in the cheese with her fork.

"Is there something wrong?" the waitress asks.

"No, everything's delicious," the mother says.

"I'm ordering a magician for the party," her mother says on the phone later that day. "It was going to be a surprise, but I know you don't like surprises. He does card tricks. He's expert at blending in with the guests. Everyone loves him. I have the guest list ready when you want to go over it."

They do not discuss the daughter, whether her name will or will not be on the guest list.

A daffodil is missing from a garden.

The stone is missing from a chalked hopscotch game.

"It's time," the husband says, waking her at three one morning. For a moment the mother thinks she has gone into labor with her missing daughter and is waking her husband. She must have been dreaming, which means she must have fallen asleep.

"What," she says. "Time for what?"

"I ordered an alarm system," her husband says. "I just wanted to let you know before you saw the charge."

"Fine," the mother says, rolling away toward the wall and squeezing her eyes shut. Her husband sits on the side of their bed. She can feel him watching her and deepens her breathing. Finally she hears him walk away, his slippers padding across the carpet.

The next morning it's Sunday, and she gets in her car while he is in the downstairs office, the door cracked open, the steady clicking of his fingers on the keys. "Yep," he says to no one. "Tell me about it."

She is wearing what she hopes are nondenominational church clothes, a long skirt and peasant blouse. Flat sandals. When she gets there, the service has already started. She sits down in a white folding chair toward the back and listens to the sermon about forgiveness. She recognizes the minister from his picture online. His wire-rimmed glasses and thinning blond hair.

She wishes people kneeled in this church. She would like to feel the hard floor under her knees. Someone is reaching for her hand. They are singing together, holding hands. "No greater love," the man next to her sings in his grandfather baritone, his thick fingers pressing between hers.

"I lost my daughter," the mother says to him when the song is over and they are walking to the lobby where there is coffee and cookies.

"Maybe I can help you find her," the man says. "Sometimes the kids like to play out back."

"Maybe so," the mother says, but she's already out the front door and running to her car in her flat sandals, the back straps slipping down her heels.

When she gets home, she sees her husband hammering a large white wooden sign into their front lawn. For a moment she thinks he's putting their house up for sale, that they're moving, and their daughter will never find them if she comes home. But the sign is two eyes with the words *We're Watching* written beneath them in black Halloween faux scary print.

"What do you think?" the husband says. "We ordered them made for the whole neighborhood. Anyone who wants one can have one at cost."

The mother reaches for her husband's hand, the one that doesn't have the hammer in it. Together they study the sign in their yard, the eyes cartoonish and wide.

"It was a very good deal," the husband says, "ordering in bulk."

"My mother is planning a party for us," the mother says. "Twenty-five years. There will be special olives. For the martinis."

"That should do it," the husband says. "Until the security system is in."

She wants to ask him if he thinks the thief is one person or many, if there's a pattern to the crimes, a tricycle on Monday, a tennis shoe on Tuesday, a doormat on Wednesday.

"Do you want to know where I've been?" she asks.

"No," he says. Or she thinks that's what he says. Maybe he said yes. An airplane is flying low over their house now and blocking out their conversation.

The mother takes her hand back and waves at the plane like she's trying to wave down a bus that's already left the stop. "Down here!" she shouts.

"Please."

"Don't forget us."

Remodel

When the man across the street comes to check on the progress on his house, I go over there and tell him I'm divorcing my husband. "Too bad we won't be neighbors much longer," I say, "now that your house is almost done."

He stares at his new wall skeptically. It's low to the ground and leans to one side. A distressed brick is loose.

"It already looks old," I say.

"That's what we were going for," he says. "Authentic."

"I used to look better," I say.

He's still staring at the wall but he nods. Maybe he's listening to me, or maybe he's just nodding. Maybe he heard the word *it* instead of *I* and thinks I'm insulting his wall.

"When we first moved in," I say, "*I* looked better. I was so young."

Now he turns and faces me. "You let yourself go," he says.

"Well, your wife is no charmer either," I say.

"She lost forty pounds. No carbs," he says.

"She's still hardly what I'd call thin," I say.

"You've got a point," he says.

I follow him around to the front of his house, and we squint at their new front porch, which slopes noticeably downhill as if the whole house wants to walk away from itself.

"It's designed for the rainwater to run off," he says.

I wonder for a minute what it would be like to be married to a man who has answers before you even have questions.

"But the porch is covered," I say.

"You've got a point," he says.

Way too many years have gone by for me to ask this man his name now. I remember introducing myself when we were new and his house was actually old and nondescript, not remodeled and pretending to be old and charming. I had a baby on my hip, a toddler on a big wheel rolling down the block. I had tried to be polite to this man and keep my son within eyeshot at the same time and had heard nothing he said.

"My kids are all in school now," I say. "My husband googles Mother Teresa when he's supposed to be working."

"Does she help him?" he asks.

"She's dead," I say.

"Right," he says.

"He's not even religious," I say. "He's supposed to be researching contacts for his business. Medical supplies," I add.

"Maybe you expect too much," my neighbor says. "Maybe that's your problem."

"Don't tell your wife about the divorce," I say. "It's kind of a surprise."

"I wouldn't call it a surprise," he says. "You know we're not deaf over here."

Now my neighbor is looking right at me. With the afternoon sun glinting off his silver hair, he looks like the kind of aging movie star who might play a priest or a sea captain on a made-for-TV movie.

A car passes by and then another one while we look at each other. This feels like a game of chicken, who will blink first, and I don't feel like losing.

"Aren't you renters?" my neighbor finally asks. "The wife and I never thought you'd stay this long."

"Everyone yells," I say. I think about their house, how silent it was before the hammers and drills and saws let loose, the way he calls his wife "the wife."

"Almost everyone," I add. "Normal people."

"You could at least shut your windows," he says. "It's been a relief being gone during the remodel."

"Well, la-tee-da for you," I say. Then I turn and cross the street just in time to nearly get myself hit by a car.

At back-to-school night Kyle and I sit on opposite sides of the classroom on little chairs. We're in a circle, and only the teacher is sitting on a regular-sized chair. I am sitting next to a woman with long, tan legs, and my husband is staring at the woman's legs while Mrs. Ettleman is going over the daily schedule.

The woman next to me crosses her legs, and her knee nearly hits her in her chin. She smiles at me when Mrs. Ettleman says the word "recess."

"Tom's favorite subject," she whispers.

I smile quickly and look slightly beyond her, as if I'm studying an important chart on the wall. *There Are No Stupid Questions!* I read on one of the many inspirational posters with which Mrs. Ettleman has decorated her third-grade classroom.

I'm worried about this new teacher who is obviously inexperienced in fielding questions from eight-year-olds. Each night at bedtime Hayley stalls with lists of inane questions: *What's your favorite color? Which of my Barbies do you like best? What would you eat if you could only eat one food ever?*

Across the room, my husband is writing down notes now. He looks like a reasonable person, not like someone who spends his free time googling Mother Teresa and selling our son's old Pokémon card collection on eBay. Catching Kyle from this distance reminds me of spotting Hayley or William when they were still breastfeeding, finally detached from my body, playing with a piece of Tupperware on the kitchen floor as if they'd never needed me for an instant.

"Cute guy," the woman next to me whispers, moving her chin slightly in my husband's direction. "I'm Carol," she says.

Mrs. Ettleman is staring at us now, and I hope she's not going to use us as an example of how her elaborate warning system works. I had thought about being a teacher, had gone as far as to imagine my own classroom full of little chairs and desks.

It was part of my exit strategy, but then I looked up on my laptop how many units I still needed to take and sunk back into the living room couch.

"I bet he's gay," I whisper back.

"All the good ones," she says.

And then we both turn back to Mrs. Ettleman and pretend to focus.

After Mrs. Ettleman finishes her presentation, Kyle and I easily lose each other in the general chaos of exiting parents. I walk home quickly, determined to reach our front door first.

"William's in his room," Hayley says. Hayley is sitting on the living room floor building a house of cards, using Kyle's poker chips for pillars.

I knock at William's locked door, and he opens it just enough so he can poke his head out. "I'm doing homework," he says.

I wonder if my son will turn into the kind of husband who answers questions before his wife asks them.

"Just checking," I say as his door shuts.

I go back downstairs and ask Hayley what she thinks of Tom.

"Tom was there?" she says. My daughter is only eight, but she is blushing.

"His mother," I say.

She goes back to her cards. I look closely and see that it's not a house she's building but a whole development of little attached houses.

"He's okay, I guess," she says, balancing the edges of a six of hearts over blue poker-chip pillars.

But it's too late. I have seen her future, longing after boys who love recess more than anything.

"Daddy!" Hayley is up and running toward the door, and then she is in his arms being flung around in the air.

"Did you get lost on the way home?" I ask.

"Come look at my prison," Hayley says when Kyle finally puts her down. "I made a little cell for everyone who does anything bad."

"Well, would you look at that," Kyle says. "Aren't you clever."

"I thought you were building condos," I say.

But no one is listening to me. Hayley and Kyle are talking about nachos and beer and lemonade, and then they are walking back toward the kitchen together. Upstairs, I hear William laughing into his cell phone. I lean forward and blow like it's my birthday and I've just made a very important wish. I watch the card roofs skid across the top of the prison until all the ceilings are wide open.

"Minimum security," I say to the invisible convicts. "Everyone is free to go."

Tom's mother, Carol, and I show up to volunteer at the same time the next day, and Mrs. Ettleman tells us we were supposed to alternate Wednesdays. "Was the sign-up sheet confusing?" she asks.

"Oh, I'm sure it was my fault," Carol says. "I never pay enough attention to these things."

I see now that she's standing that Carol has a thick waist, or maybe her waist only looks thick because of her long, thin legs. Still, it's a relief to see her this way, her thick waist, confused about the day, that this is the kind of woman my husband stares at across a classroom.

"It could have been anyone's fault," Mrs. Ettleman says.

Mrs. Ettleman smiles at me, and instead of playing nice, I listen to the silence in the classroom. Outside the door, the children are talking, lining up, back from recess, Tom's favorite subject, while Mrs. Ettleman and I stare at each other.

"It was pretty clear from the sign-up sheet that today was my Wednesday," I say.

"Would it kill you to be nicer?" Kyle would say. "Give it a rest."

"I know what. I'll just put you both to work!" Mrs. Ettleman finally says.

The children come in and sit down, but they're jittery, flushed and hyped up from the playground. Mrs. Ettleman tells them to get out their journals.

"Time to write about our thoughts," Mrs. Ettleman says. "Whatever's on your mind. Remember, don't judge. All of your thoughts matter."

Right, I think. Of course.

It's easy to find Tom. Even seated, he's a head taller than my daughter. He's bouncing a fat pink eraser on his knee like it's a soccer ball while Hayley bends over her work, writing in her tiny, neat handwriting that will get her nowhere in life.

Mrs. Ettleman gives us a pile of papers and leads us out to the volunteer table in the hallway. Once again we are in little chairs with Tom's mother's long legs folded up. We're supposed to check off who's turned in their homework, and Carol is moving through her pile way too quickly, drawing messy red stars on top of each paper, oblivious to the whole reason for volunteering, to see firsthand how your child stacks up against her classmates.

"Guess who I walked home with?" Carol says, checking off my daughter's assignment without even taking note of her properly punctuated sentences.

"Home?" I say.

"From back-to-school night. Well, not really home, but he walked me to my car. You're definitely wrong about someone being gay," she adds. "You know, this is fun. I'm glad we got mixed up and got to volunteer together."

"How do you know?" I ask. "Did he ask you out? Did he kiss you?"

"Not with all those parents walking by."

"Then how do you know?" I say, leaning so hard on my pencil that I feel the tip of it press through the paper to the work table.

"You're hilarious," Tom's mother says. "As if a girl can't tell."

The next paper in my pile is Tom's. Although I long to circle every mistake in it myself, I hand it to Carol. "Maybe you want to check this one," I say.

"He's in medical supplies," Carol says, scrawling a red star on top of Tom's paper. "Very lucrative."

As I walk up the hill to my house, I see the man who lives across the street. He's back again, staring at his little wall. I think about pretending to talk on my cell phone, laughing into it the way my son does at night when his door is shut and he's alone with his private world of homework and friends. But instead I walk right up to my neighbor.

"You know, I don't think you should judge," I say. "When you've never had children, you have no idea."

"You may be the most self-absorbed person I've ever met," he says.

"I never think about myself," I say.

"Then maybe you just don't think," he says. "When Eugene died, you didn't even send a card," he says. "All of the other neighbors had their casseroles and dessert plates and carnations, and you had nothing."

I look at my neighbor, searching his face for a clue.

"For god's sake. It was on the front page of the newspaper. Seven years ago. Right on the football field during training, nobody even tackling him. Just plain asthma. His first year away at college. He was allergic to Michigan. Different grasses."

I try to think back seven years, Hayley starting to walk, William in kindergarten. "I thought you were having a party and we weren't invited," I say. "Because we were new. Because we were renters. Because you didn't like us."

"I didn't know you well enough not to like you then," he says. "The wall's a disappointment. It's not the way I imagined it at all," he adds.

"I'm sorry. I didn't know," I say. "I don't remember ever seeing your son before."

"Everyone knew," he says.

I watch my neighbor get in his car and drive off.

I stare at my own house across the street, the front yard that needs watering, the tree that William doesn't climb anymore. I'm not used to the quiet after months of trucks and drilling and hammering, but the builders haven't been here in days. I wonder if my neighbor fired them and plans to start the remodel all over again. The air smells sour, like low tide, and the quiet feels vaguely alarming, the kind of single perfect moment right before an earthquake hits.

Night Shift

I don't know exactly what I expected when I started dating the nurse. Maybe a little white outfit, a stethoscope splayed open around her neck. Something between a French maid and a veterinarian, I guess, if you pressed me.

I'll tell you what I didn't expect: the way Val cupped one of my testicles the first time we slept together, weighing it in her hand as if it were a piece of ham she was thinking about buying. "Christ, I see body parts all the time," she said to me when I flinched. "You can save the modesty."

Val was my first nurse. What the hell did I know. I wasn't even sure if I'd call her again. Although she picked up extra money working the ERs on occasional weekends, I knew her because she was the school nurse at the high school where I taught. And if I didn't call her, I can tell you one thing: there would be no more lunch hours spent making out on the sick cot, surrounded by posters of graphic tours of the inner ear and digestive track. It was back to the teacher's lounge for me.

My daughter was due soon for her every-other-weekend visit, and I thought about introducing her to the nurse, her being a kind of walking first aid kit and all and how this might not be such a bad thing. Karina was five and accident prone. My ex-wife and I had to alternate emergency rooms to throw the social worker patrol off. Hell, we never even spanked her. Who would break a kid's arm, is what I want to know. What sort of sick fuck would crack such small ribs?

I told the nurse about Karina on our first real date after the testicle incident. "Val," I said. "I've got a daughter I'd like you to meet."

"I was wondering when we'd get to that," she said.

We were eating exotically named pizza at one of those places where you have to pay so much you might as well be eating steak. Still, I liked the way Val ate, one or two bites at a time until she was full, not like some girls I had dated, all delicate napkin dabbing.

"It was the bath toys," she said. "A dead giveaway." Val shook garlic powder across the remaining pizza that sat between us. "Now we'll be even," she said. "For later."

The word *later* filled me with anticipation and dread. It was midweek, a good TV night. I wondered if there might be a way to drop Val straight off at home. "She's accident prone," I said. "My daughter."

"The first thing we need to look at," Val said, "is the childproofing situation."

After dinner, I double-parked in front of a hardware store while Val shopped. She came out carrying a lumpy white plastic bag in each hand. "Supplies," she said, sliding in and slamming her door shut behind her.

While I followed her around trying to come up with suggestions to offer, Val childproofed my apartment. I thought about pointing out that Karina was five, not two, but just last visit I had caught my daughter thoughtfully pointing a salad fork at an electrical socket as if measuring the possibilities.

When Val was through with my apartment, she started on my balcony rails, stretching netting across. "I'm ready for my beer now," she said, twisting the last of the ties shut. I drank one with her while we watched the cars pull in and out of the parking lot. I had the cheapest apartment available in my building, no view, no screens around the balcony to keep out bugs. When I rented it, I felt lucky anyone would rent me anything, as if I were on the run from the law, not just my wife and daughter.

The thing about my wife was she tried so hard, there was no way I could keep living with her after Karina came along. Before Karina, her botched efforts to make herself into a grown-up seemed endearing. I'd come home from the high school where I taught five sections of Math for Misfits, the commonly known name for Math 111, Developmental Algebra, and find appliquéd flowers on our headboard, Cornish game hens cooling on the kitchen counter. It didn't matter that the flowers were blurred at the edges or the white paper socks she put on the game hens had singed. In my mind, I gave her an "A" for effort.

But after Karina came along, I had to lower my grade. I'd find piles of baby magazines dog-eared by the toilet, whole squash wedged tight in the Cuisinart feeder, and the kind of depressing classical music I associated with old men driving Buicks blaring out of our stereo system. "C," I'd think when I walked in. "C-minus," I'd decide when I'd find Karina screaming in her crib while Stephanie hand-washed cloth diapers in the kitchen sink.

After I left her, Stephanie traded in her attempts at domesticity for good causes. She let her roots go brown and cut her nails straight across. Each time she dropped Karina off and drove away, I'd see a new bumper sticker glued to the back of her car. I tried to keep up but usually I blew it, offering her a hamburger when she was off meat, my teacher's discount tickets to the circus when she was saving elephants.

Although I liked the way the nurse ate, I wasn't wild about the way she drank beer, making what seemed to me an exaggerated *Aah* sound after each deep swallow. How some men jacked off over photos in magazines was beyond me. Who could tell anything about a woman he hadn't sat down for a meal with? "Ready to call it a day?" Val said.

While I was still thinking about whether or not I wanted to sleep with Val that night, the negotiation of mattress space and pillows versus the singular way Val had of making me feel in bed, supremely on edge yet somehow in the care of a dedicated public servant, she was already headed out my front door, her hand tightly squeezing my newly childproofed doorknob cover. "Work tomorrow," she said. "School night."

Stephanie and Karina both showed up Saturday morning, their ponytails pulled back tight. Their ears stuck out in similar optimistic-looking ways I'd never noticed before. "We're growing it out for the Alopecia Society," Stephanie said. "Don't even think about taking her for a haircut."

"Wigs," Stephanie said when I stared at her.

"For bald people," Karina added.

They tended to treat me collectively like my most dismal kind of student, slow-witted and doddering. Although all of my students were failures, in truth, I preferred the troublemakers, the ones who sold powders and pills and bags of pot out of the glove compartments of their ridiculously souped-up Pontiacs. At least they seemed to have a few ideas, however clichéd and misguided.

"Gotcha!" I said a little too loudly. There were things I wanted to ask, like would they simply cut the ponytails off or cut in closer to the scalp? Shouldn't I, Karina's father, have a say in the whole business? But I had learned to choose my battles.

"See you Sunday, Sweetie," Stephanie said, kissing Karina on her forehead.

And then the two of us were alone. It was always like this for the first few minutes, Karina looking around my apartment as if there might be someone she knew better and was more anxious to see just around the corner and me feeling as if I had suddenly been given guardianship of a remote relative's child. There was something unnatural about all of it, fathers left alone with their children. We'd eye each other in Denny's and Pizza Hut, the divorced weekend dads, sizing up each other's deficiencies. Usually I had something ready to break the ice with when Karina got there, Popsicles or a jar of bubbles or butterscotch pudding, but my new dating life had thrown me off course and I hadn't been to a store all week. I didn't even have milk in the refrigerator. "How about we go shopping?" I said.

Karina looked too big for it after I put her in the ride-on section of the shopping cart, but I wasn't sure how to gracefully admit to my mistake so I left her there, pushing my oversized baby around the store and asking her advice about brands while I picked out cereal and ice cream and frozen pizza.

"The store Mom goes to has these little carts kids can push themselves," Karina said, alternately bouncing her feet off the cart and me.

"That sounds cool," I said.

"This kind of hurts my butt. Get skim, not two percent," Karina said. "That's what Mom gets. It's better for you."

I broke the red licorice open while we waited in the checkout line and pretended to smoke it. And, finally, here it was, our ice-breaker moment, appearing on its own accord. "Darling," Karina said, blowing a thin line of air into my face. "Baby face," I blew back.

The nurse was waiting for us when we got back, standing outside my apartment building, holding a small brown dog that looked, if not completely diseased, at least aggressively neglected, its fur matted in sections, missing in others. "Who have we got here?" I said.

"I'm calling him Buster," Val said. She leaned over toward me and continued in a whisper. "He's a weekend loaner puppy, from the pound. Trial period, they call it."

"Can I hold him?" Karina asked.

"Sure, I guess so," I said, mouthing the word *shots?* to Val, who nodded.

Carrying the grocery bags, I followed Karina and Val up the stairs. Below her shorts, the top of Karina's thighs were red and pinched-looking from where she was squeezed into the shopping cart. Tomorrow there would be bruises.

"It's like carrying a rabbit," she said to Val. "It's like carrying a lunch box. I think he peed on me."

"Every child needs a pet to learn responsibility," she said, taking Buster back. "Maybe it's time for his walk."

After Karina washed her arms and changed her shirt, we tried to take Buster on a walk around the block. He took small, halting steps and stopped often just to sit. I had never walked in my neighborhood before. It wasn't that kind of place. It was the kind of place people drove through on their way somewhere else. But now we were forced to stop with Buster and take in the scenery, which, frankly, wasn't much. More apartment buildings like mine, flat-faced and beige. It was the kind of place where people lived until their real lives began. Val wore a tank top, and when I got tired of pretending to take in the scenery, I silently counted the freckles on the back of her shoulders.

The truth was, though, that Val was on to something. I had never seen Karina looking as blissed-out as she did walking Buster. "Buster, Buster, my little Buster Bar," she said, kneeling down and rubbing his sad little head each time he stopped for a breather.

Halfway around the block, Val finally reached down, picked Buster up, and said, "What do you say we head back now."

While Val and Karina gave Buster a bath, I sat at the kitchen table and worked on my letter to my neighbor across the hall. She was giving a piano lesson as she did all weekend long, and through my front door I could make out a male laugh and a rudimentary attempt at the first pitched notes of "Für Elise." Her students were all adults and all men as far as I could tell. I'd hear them pounding their way up our stairs each weekend, smell their aftershave outside my door, find an occasional cigarette stamped out but still smoldering on our shared landing.

While the piano teacher and I had only been on one actual date together, we had had several odd make-out sessions in the hallway before and after this date, one or the other of our bags of groceries at our feet, and now that I was dating the nurse I felt a need to explain myself to her. *Dear Neighbor*, each of my attempts began and ended. I was certain she had given me her name, but I couldn't remember it, and I had only the last name on her mailbox to go on. The name Doris came to mind but didn't feel quite right. While hardly irresistible in other ways, my neighbor wore a tiny stud in her tongue that, when it found its way into my mouth, bent my toes with yearning.

"Here we are, all spic and span," Val said, and I folded my letter in half. Buster's fur looked patchier, but his eyes did seem less rheumy. My daughter held him against her chest, and as I waited for her to ask if we could keep him, I began to prepare my speech about the no-pet clauses at both her mother's and my apartments.

"I know he has to go back," Karina said. "But Val said maybe he could spend the night."

"Affection and responsibility," Val said. "Two of the key components to a successful adult life."

"He can sleep in my bed," Karina said. "You won't even know he's here."

"Night shift," Val said and headed toward the door. "I'll come check on you guys in the a.m."

After Val left, we fed Buster skim milk and a can of tuna fish, Karina's head on the ground next to the can. She pretended to chew while the dog ate, as if the dog needed encouragement or a role model. Then without even asking for a story, Karina took the dog and they both licked my cheek good night and went to bed.

I sat back at the kitchen table and worked on my letter some more. When it was finally right, I walked across the hallway and stuck it under the piano teacher's door. But before I could even make it back to my apartment, she had opened her door and was waving me to come in, something I'd always avoided up until now. It was bad enough she lived across the hall. Seeing the inside of a woman's apartment was way too detailed for me, like knowing if she shaved her legs all the way up or stopped at her knees. "What have we got here?" my neighbor said. "Shall we read this together?"

I followed her in and sat on her couch, staring at her lacquered piano and the framed posters she'd hung over it, posters that advertised art shows in Paris and Madrid, places I sincerely doubted she'd ever been.

"I hope you're a crème de menthe fan," she said. "It's all I seem to have in the house."

She sat next to me on the couch and handed me a glass of thick, phlegmy-looking green liquid and watched me drink. It coated my throat like cough syrup, and I fought back the urge to gag.

"Where's yours?" I asked her.

She waved my question away. "That's all I had left," she said, unfolding my letter and reading it. "You go on and enjoy it." She folded my letter back up and handed it to me. "You're breaking up with me? I didn't even know we were dating."

"I'm sort of new at this," I said. I finished my drink and put my empty glass on her coffee table and got up before I gave in to my urge to feel her studded tongue in my mouth. I put out my hand, and she looked at it. "See you around, then?" I said.

After I left, I stood on the landing between our two front doors for a few minutes and listened. I thought maybe she'd play something to indicate her mood, a ballad of some kind or perhaps the soaring theme music to a romantic movie. But instead all I heard was the television set click on.

The next morning the nurse showed up still in uniform. The only uniform I'd seen her in up until now was her school uniform, a thick white dress with a smile button pinned to the collar to reassure the students. I'd never seen her this way before in her serious green ER gear, and I hated to admit there was anything erotic about any of it. Because my daughter was there, I made myself stare at her clunky white shoes and think about IVs and bedpans. Karina and I were eating breakfast, and the dog was still asleep in Karina's bed. Karina had a new scratch from wrestling with the dog that ran from her elbow to her wrist. I blamed Val for it.

"How's our little pup?" she said.

We all tiptoed in and looked at him. He was sleeping at the foot of Karina's bed in a damp spot too large to be drool. "You didn't walk him," Val said. "Affection AND responsibility."

It was one thing to lecture me, but my daughter was only five, and, besides, she was already slated to be scalped. "My fault entirely, Val," I said, pulling off the sheets and blanket and piling them on the floor. "Come on, little guy, let's get a move on." I woke Buster, carried the dog downstairs, set him on the ground, and waited while he sniffed around a small circle. I decided we had been dead wrong. There was nothing puppy-like about him. Buster was a decrepit old man.

While Val took a nap on Karina's mattress, Karina dictated a letter to me to send back to the pound with Buster, her speech carefully modulated as if she was attempting to read the words she was dictating. *I am a loveable dog*, I wrote. *Please take me home soon.*

When Stephanie came to pick Karina up, I hid the dog in the back room where the nurse was still sleeping. I knew kids and parents weren't supposed to form secret pacts together, but I didn't know how to explain Buster, so I made Karina promise to keep him between us. If he wasn't adopted yet, I promised her we could take him for another weekend visit. I didn't mention the other possibilities, what else might happen to Buster in the meantime.

"Well, I guess I'm not good enough for the Alopecia people," Stephanie said as she ran her fingers through Karina's hair. "It seems they don't want anything processed."

"Bad break," I said, but secretly I hoped that this might mean Karina could hold onto her hair, too.

"The pamphlet stated this was just a clarification, but I can tell you this, no one ever mentioned anything about a problem with a perm when I called in the first place. Jesus, you'd think they'd be grateful for anything."

I walked Stephanie and Karina out to the parking lot and slowly climbed up my stairs behind a middle-aged man who I suspected looked a lot like me from behind. There was no mistaking what he was humming under his breath, the *denuh, denuh, denuh* of the introduction to "Für Elise."

We turned in opposite directions on the landing, and I opened my front door and, suddenly as exhausted as if I, too, had worked the night shift, went inside to crawl in next to my sleeping nurse. Our borrowed dog was spending the last few hours of his weekend retreat at the foot of Karina's bed, and I was careful to let him sleep, to fold my legs up toward my chest, so I didn't accidentally kick him awake.

I suspected my nurse was a practiced sleeper, but I touched the side of her face anyway, ran a finger over her cheek to see if that would do anything. I saw how I might stop calling her altogether or how we might breed dogs or build houses or sponsor a foreign exchange student. When she woke, I'd ask her to think through the possibilities.

Viola

When Carmen plays viola, she feels love soar down through the veins in her arm, and she pushes it through her bow. When her father's heart stopped last year, the pain began in his shoulder and etched its way down his arm, but he didn't let the pain out because he didn't know what it was, what was being asked of him.

People say it's a mystery, this kind of love, that it's unconditional, but people are wrong. Carmen wishes this weren't the case. She wishes that she and Jesus could have forgiven her father for the girl at the office who sent him out on his construction jobs. But her father never asked for forgiveness, and even Jesus requires that much.

Her father left his cell phone in the kitchen drawer when he was home, forgot about it while her mother cleaned houses and he napped on the couch or pulled weeds from the potted tomato plants he kept on the balcony. But even on vibrate, Carmen could hear his phone in the drawer when she got home from school, and she went to it. She hated to give the calls to her father, but the calls meant money. "Put him on," the girl would say over Carmen's long silences, her voice reedy and crisp and smelling like mint even over phone. "Give him to me."

Carmen divides the world up into orchestra and band. The girl who sent her father out on construction jobs and texted photos of herself over the phone that Carmen is sure would have shocked even the middle school boys who drew penises on the inside covers of pre-algebra textbooks was band. She was a trombone or maybe snare drum. Something showy and loud. Carmen worried about her appearing at her father's funeral. She had only seen pictures of her on the small screen of her father's cell phone, but Carmen knew she'd recognize her. She imagined the church doors opening and the girl surrounded by thick gusts of air, her hair blown back around her face, her thick, pouty lips pink and wet.

The girl was marching band, Carmen decided as she scanned the church, twisted around in the front pew, looking over the heads of her uncles and aunts and cousins. She had already moved on.

Carmen likes orchestra rehearsal, but she doesn't like Jenna, the first-chair violin Carmen is seated next to every Tuesday and Thursday. Carmen has heard one of her uncles say that he smells money when he goes to the racetrack, that that's how he picks his horses. When Jenna leans over her violin with her clean blond hair cut into thick layers that fall around her face, Carmen smells money, which, she decides, is cinnamon mixed with chlorine and talcum powder. Jenna wears white sneakers and small gold earrings and chews gum so quietly that she's never asked to spit it out, even in French class where Madame Toulec walks up and down the aisles with her tiny pink trash can in one hand and violet-scented tissues in the other.

The door to the music room opens as they are finishing rehearsing Bach's Brandenburg 3. "I have donuts," a boy in the doorway, someone's little brother, says. This is a difficult piece, and they aren't even close to getting it right yet. They need to run through it again in parts and then from the beginning. The second violin section is coming in a beat too late. One of the cellos is hitting a B instead of a B-sharp. As first-chair violin, it's Jenna's job to lead them, but Jenna is a terrible leader. She is already laughing and folding up her sheet music. Carmen looks to Mr. Korman for backup, but he's doing crossword puzzles at his desk in his little office attached to the rehearsal space and not looking up.

The boy has let himself into the music room now. He's wearing a baseball uniform and carrying a big white bag with handles. Carmen thinks of her own little brother who is probably this boy's age, eight maybe, or nine, but smaller, not just shorter. Her brother's ears stick out a little too much and his long, dark bangs hang over his eyes. All of the other little brothers at Henry

Middle School have spiky blond hair and noses peeling from sunburns, and they're dressed for baseball or soccer or basketball. They kick rocks across the playground and high-five the most popular eighth-grade boys, the ones that Carmen has trouble looking in the eye when they are forced into group work together in history class. Carmen's brother comes home after school, puts on his pajamas and watches cartoons in Spanish. He hides behind their mother's leg when they are somewhere new.

The little brothers at Henry Middle School are band.

Carmen's little brother is orchestra.

Now that donuts are here, everyone has stopped playing. They do not know their music, and the bell hasn't rung yet, but class is apparently over. Carmen had expected more from her new school, has trouble accepting that the students here are in just as much of a hurry to get out of class as they were at Susan B. Anthony. That the only difference is that they all speak English, and so far no one appears to be pregnant.

Jenna lets her violin fall onto the carpet that's so thin you can see through it in places. Carmen listens to the sounds of the strings tumbling all around her, the accidental notes that let out when a cello falls into a bass, the metal thud of a music stand being kicked over.

Maybe this is the sound of money, she thinks.

Carmen holds tight to her viola, which isn't hers at all, really, but on loan from Henry Middle the way her old one was on loan from Susan B. Anthony Middle.

In truth, Carmen would like a donut, but she will not join the orchestra, knocking each other out of the way to be the first to reach into the bag.

"We're not done," Carmen says instead.

"Fuck you," Luke says. Luke plays cello, but to Carmen he will always be band. He curses often and in a disarmingly good-natured way. Carmen is devoted to him secretly and completely.

She is as protective of her love for him as she is of her loaned viola, aware that neither will ever be hers.

She is a transfer student from across town, making the switch this year when a slot opened on the waiting list her mother put her on when a seventh grader at her old school got pregnant. The principal mailed home a rare note in English and Spanish, encouraging parents to discuss both abstinence and birth control with their children. Instead, Carmen's mother decided she should go to another school, one in the same neighborhood where she cleans houses.

Carmen has no one at Henry Middle School to confide in about Luke. Her friends from her old school called her stuck up and then stopped returning her text messages after she transferred. Carmen is alone with her feelings, which, she decides, makes her closer to Jesus, who was also alone, despite his great love for humanity

Mr. Korman is out of his office now, saying, "Save one for me. Take it easy there, kids." Mr. Korman has a big belly that hangs over his belt, but from the back he looks thin. Each time he turns around his belly is an unhappy surprise to Carmen, like the Sunday school teacher she once had with the long, smooth dyed-blond hair and brown face full of wrinkles.

"Going, going, gone," Mr. Korman says, reaching deep into the white bag.

A half hour later, Carmen is alone in the music room with her viola. She is not really allowed to be in this classroom alone, but Mr. Korman trusts her to lock up behind her. All of the teachers trust her at her new middle school, just like they trusted her at her old middle school and at her elementary school before that. She is the girl who takes the attendance down to the main office and walks the sick boy to the nurse's room. The girl who copies down the homework assignment from the board and never asks for an extension. At her old school, she didn't talk to the other girls in Advisory class about cramps and stealing cigarettes, and at her new school, she doesn't talk to them about skipping math tutoring and making out with high school boys. She is the girl who gets the certificate at the end of each marking period for never being tardy or absent.

Carmen is alone with her viola, the most misunderstood of instruments. Even the man at the music store where she buys her replacement strings pronounces it wrong. *Vi-ola* instead of *vee-ola*.

Her father didn't know what she played. *My daughter the violin player*, he used to brag to relatives at parties. Correcting him felt mean, like correcting his double negatives or the way he said the number three as if it didn't have an "h" in it. *Viola*, she said, under her breath. *Viola, viola, viola.*

Her parents are from El Salvador and learned English from the channel nine news, the world's problems in the background whenever they were home. She didn't forgive her father for the girl on the cell phone, but she forgave him for not knowing the difference between a violin and a viola.

Once, looking in the music section of the bookstore, Carmen came across an entire book of viola jokes, and she felt shame radiate through her body while she read each page, committing jokes to memory. *How do you keep your violin from getting stolen? Put it in a viola case. What's the difference between a viola and a trampoline? You take your shoes off to jump on a trampoline.*

In truth, when Carmen chose the viola as her instrument in fourth grade, she didn't know what she was picking from the "petting zoo" set up in the cafeteria. Embarrassed to try instruments without already knowing how to play, Carmen had pointed when it came to her turn. *We finally have our viola player. Excellent*, the music teacher said, making a note on her clipboard.

Carmen had learned to appreciate its sound later. The viola didn't squeal the way the violins did when you played a bad note. You didn't have to stand it up in public in front of you and wrap your arm around it the way you did a cello.

Mr. Korman thinks she stays in the music room to practice her viola. And she does, going over and over her scales. But she really stays to dance in the center of the empty room. Carmen has thick ankles, slightly bowed legs and slumped posture. She knows all of these things about herself. Her family never had money for dance lessons, and even if they had, Carmen wouldn't have asked for them. She doesn't want to pull pink tights over her thick ankles and learn what she's doing wrong. She doesn't want to line up next to girls who look like Jenna. She wants to dance alone.

When Carmen is sure that enough time has passed that even the principal has left for the day, she places her viola in the red velvet lining of its case. Ever since her father died and she knelt before him laid out in his coffin, she has thought of the violin's case as its coffin, and she crosses herself before snapping it shut. *What's the difference between a viola and a coffin? The coffin has the dead person on the inside.*

There is a pile of old classical records in Mr. Korman's office on the floor near his desk. Carmen pulls out *The Nutcracker* from the center where she left it last week, the frayed edge of its jacket sticking out a little. Carmen's uncle has a broken record player in his garage, but Mr. Korman is the only person she knows who still has a turntable that actually works. Sometimes when he gets tired of sitting in his office and doing crossword puzzles and listening to how terrible the students sound, he comes out and yells at them and then plays Vivaldi or Mozart or Schumann, and tells them to shut up and listen. That this is how it's done.

"Don't ever touch my turntable," he tells the class every time he plays them a record. "Do you know how expensive it is to replace a damn needle?"

You've got to update, Mr. Korman, Jenna always says, but Carmen likes the way the records sound, crackled and serious.

Carmen knows exactly where "The Dance of the Sugar Plum Fairies" is on the record. She takes off her shoes and socks and finds the thick groove and gently places the arm down so the needle is in the right spot. Then she folds her body over itself in the center of the room and listens. She tries to pick out each of the instruments one at a time: trumpet, oboe, flute, violin, until she finally hones in on the viola section.

But no matter how hard she listens, every instrument, not just the violas, is overshadowed by the celesta. Carmen wrote a research paper on this piece for extra credit and knows the ethereal bell-like sound is made by tiny hammers striking metal plates, that this particular sound is a result of careful engineering. But it still sounds like heaven to Carmen each time she hears it. And, each time, she thinks about her father and wonders if he made it there, even though he cheated on her mother with the cell phone girl, even though he never asked anyone, not even Carmen, for forgiveness.

Carmen rises on her tiptoes, arches her arms over her head and spins slowly around. She imagines her father and then Jesus watching her, seeing her beauty, the way she feels this music coursing through her body. She imagines Luke, the cello player, staring at her with desire. What she doesn't imagine is the boy with the donuts standing once again in the doorway.

"What are you doing?" he asks.

Carmen stops dancing, but the record is spinning, and she can feel the sugar plum fairies still dancing all around her.

"Nothing," she says.

"I saw you," the boy says.

"What do you want?" Carmen says. She is walking over to the record player now. She feels her bare feet moving over the thin carpet. She lifts the arm up and the music stops.

"Jenna forgot her violin," the boy says. "She's in the car, with our mom. You're not allowed to touch Mr. Korman's record player. Jenna says no one is, that he's a total freak about it."

Carmen ignores the boy and opens Jenna's locker, the combination lock open and dangling the way it always is. Carmen lifts off the lock and opens the door, then hands the boy the violin. "You're lucky I was here," she says.

"I would have just found the janitor," the boy says. "I'm going to tell you played Mr. Korman's record player when he wasn't here. Give me something, or I'm going to tell."

Carmen stares at the boy who had the bag of donuts, the little brother in the baseball uniform. He's wearing a cap now and she can't see his spiky blond hair, but now she understands that it's Jenna's hair, cut short and mean. "How do you know I didn't have permission?" Carmen says.

"Did you?"

"I don't have anything to give you," Carmen says.

"Give me five dollars, or I'm telling," the boy says.

"I don't have anything," Carmen says. It's true. Her mother won't let her bring money on the bus because it might get stolen. She only has her student ID and her prepaid bus card.

"Show me your bra," the boy says. "Show it to me, or I'm going to tell Mr. Korman that you played a record." The boy stares at her bare feet. "And I'm going to tell my sister that you're a total freak."

Carmen laughs, but the boy isn't smiling. She hears a car horn beep four times in a row. She has always been the girl the teachers trust.

"They're waiting for me," the boy says. "My mother and Jenna. They're both in the car."

"I'll bring you the money tomorrow," she says.

"Too late," the boy says. He's turning and walking toward the door when Carmen says, "Stop."

The boy is not much older than Carmen's brother. Maybe he's ten or eleven, she decides. He'll tell Mr. Korman that she used his record player, and he'll tell Jenna that he saw the transfer girl dancing around the music room, and Jenna will tell everyone, even Luke, and they'll all know. "Okay," she finally says. Carmen closes her eyes and lifts her shirt up quickly and then pulls it back down.

"Now promise not to tell," Carmen says.

"I'm not promising anything," the boy says.

Carmen hears the car horn again. Next year or the year after when he's at this middle school, Carmen will have already moved on to high school. He is capable of ruining her life only right now, at this very moment.

"Promise or I won't forgive you, and Jesus won't forgive you either," she says.

"Jenna's right," the boy says. "You are a total freak."

Someone is leaning on the car horn now. Carmen imagines Jenna's thin fingers pushing and pushing.

Carmen stares at the boy hard. "Promise," she says.

"You're crazy," the boy says, but something passes over his sunburned face that Carmen hopes is fear. "I'm coming!" the boy yells, and then he's gone.

Carmen lifts *The Nutcracker* off the turntable and puts it back in the album cover. She slips the album into the center of the pile near Mr. Korman's desk, the frayed edge sticking out just enough so she can find it next time.

When Carmen steps outside with her viola, the fog is already rolling in. She walks down the sidewalk to the bus stop, feeling the air turn wet on her arms and face, the only music in her head now the sound of a siren, someone else's emergency, moving nearer and nearer to her.

Come See Us Again

She should have labeled the baby teeth. She finds them in zip-lock sandwich bags stuffed deep into the back of her sweater drawer with the Vicodin they sent her home with from the hospital twenty years ago. Sewed tight from the unplanned C-section, she wanted to nurse her daughter, to get this one part right. She pushed away even the Tylenol her husband left by her bed with a water glass. She wouldn't let anything contaminate her milk.

Some baggies have two of her daughter's teeth in them, and the mother wonders if they fell out at the same time, although she doesn't ever remember this happening, and it seems unlikely.

She pops open the bottle. Expired for nineteen years and three months, according to the label. She takes two. She unzips a bag with one tiny yellowed tooth in it and rests the tooth on her tongue with the pills, the taste of bone and white tablets, all of it bitter and dissolving. She imagines each letter on each pill blurring onto her tongue. She feels the tooth dissolving, too, even though she knows this cannot be true. A tooth cannot dissolve. Although maybe this one can, a tooth that sat for nearly two decades in a plastic bag behind masses of unraveling sweaters. She swallows, and it's all gone already, nothing catching hold in her throat on its way down.

Her daughter was not the child who climbed over the guardrail and fell into the gorilla cage; not the child who took off running down the street when the ice cream truck turned the corner, too joyful to notice the other truck, the one full of yard sale furniture, until it was too late, the sad tinny music of the ice cream truck leaving notes like misquotes in the air. She was not the child under the truck's tire, rib and cheekbone flattened, the bed of the truck piled high with worn mattresses and scuffed dressers. Her daughter was not the one who was tugged away from shore by the alligator's clamped jaw into a pond on an otherwise predictable family vacation to Florida.

But her daughter is the one who has disappeared. Silent for two months. She is offline or not answering her mother's emails, text messages, or phone calls. She has gone back to college or not gone back to college, gone off the grid, off her mother's radar, off the rails. She has gone wispy as smoke. She will not talk to her mother because her mother had told her it was time to stop moping over a boy, that spring break was almost over, that it was time to get out of bed.

When the ice cream truck pulled up to the curb, her daughter held her hand and kept her quarters and dimes tight in the other fist. Her thoughts were on what she would choose, chocolate-covered vanilla or Creamsicle. Either one the wrong decision, something to lament as soon as the wrapper came off, before even the first bite.

"Why did you let me? I didn't want this one."

"Next time," the mother said each time. "Next time you can have the other."

"You should tell me what to do. Why don't you know what I want?"

In California, there are no fireflies. This is what the mother has denied her daughter. Empty mason jars left in the backyard, the lids loose and ready for sunset.

"Let's wash your hands," the mother said. "Look how much that ice cream dripped. Next time," the mother said. "Next time you can get the other one."

When she ran out of ideas, when all of her emails and text messages and phone calls went unanswered, the mother finally got in her car and drove to the nondenominational church one town over. She had driven by the building many times. Small and white, it looked like a church building someone might set up by a model train track next to the post office and the general store. She had read the minister's sermons online about forgiveness, and wanted to hear about forgiveness in person.

She had signed the Welcome Sheet, and now the nondenominational church calls her. A woman with a breathless voice, or maybe she's moving closer to the phone and backing away or the line is bad, or maybe the mother's own hearing has been enveloped in a Vicodin cloud. Expired but doubled up and apparently still working. The V's and I's dissolving on her tongue with the daughter's chalky yellowed tooth. The mother has no more breast milk she is worrying about the Vicodin infecting. Her breasts are thin and empty.

"I'm calling to welcome you," the woman says. "I'm from the church welcome committee."

"I'm sorry. It's hard to hear you," the mother says.

"Welcome!" the woman shouts. "To our little church."

"Thank you," the mother says. "I have to go now."

"Please come see us again," the woman says as the mother says she can't talk now and hangs up.

"This isn't a good time."

There have been many thefts in the mother's neighborhood, lately more complicated ones. A fifteen-year-old parrot is stolen from a front porch, the empty cage still locked tight. Homework disappears from a child's neatly organized folder. A neighbor comes home from work one day to find a pregnant woman floating on a pink raft, belly-up in her backyard pool. There is talk about whether this qualifies technically as a theft because the pregnant woman brought her own raft and didn't really steal anything except the ingredients to a make a drink from the neighbor's cabinet.

"What are you doing?" the neighbor asked.

"It's virgin. Don't worry," the pool thief said, raising a familiar-looking glass full of a frothy drink, an umbrella and a toothpick full of cherries floating in it.

"This isn't your pool," the neighbor said. "Is that my glass?"

"It's always empty," the woman said, paddling over to the steps and tilting the raft over just enough to empty herself out of it, the glass high above her head. "I never hear anyone swimming in it. I didn't think you'd mind. I wasn't going to keep the glass."

"I could call the police," the neighbor said.

"No need," the pregnant woman said, her belly round over her bikini bottom, taking one more sip and leaving the glass on the inside fence ledge. "I'm already gone."

"Don't forget your raft," the neighbor said, but the pregnant woman was pulling shut the back gate behind her, her raft abandoned, floating by the steps in the shallow end.

"She was always careful," the mother tells her husband after she hangs up the phone from the welcome committee and finds him in their front yard, surveying their block, his hands making binoculars around his eyes. "This isn't like her. Is it?" the mother says. "We never expected this."

"It's all there on the listserv," the mother's husband tells her. They stand in their front yard by the *We're Watching* sign the husband has hammered into their lawn, their street dotted with these signs now, slammed in at odd angles.

"Good thing we don't have a pool," the mother says. But she is thinking that maybe they should have had a pool. Her thoughts and her words don't always match. They used to match, or at least she doesn't remember them not matching.

She pictures her daughter at a hotel pool, holding tight to the side in the shallow end while all around her children screamed and threw beach balls in the air. "Let go, honey," she told her daughter. Then once, "Just swim. You had those lessons. You know how."

"No," her daughter said. Or maybe she just glared.

"It's warmer than the ocean," the mother said, sitting on the edge and dangling her feet into the water.

"I heard it was a piña colada," the husband says. "And not a virgin one either. She walked right into the kitchen and made it in their blender. She helped herself to their liquor cabinet. She used up all the grated coconut they stored in their cheese drawer in the refrigerator."

They both look down their block. The mother imagines the pregnant woman, drunk in her bikini, wandering through their neighborhood, even though this happened days ago. The mother puts a coat on her to keep her warm because the day is chilly. She dresses her in an improbable fur that falls almost to the ground, and kitten heels.

"I saved things, but I didn't really keep track," the mother says. "The way I should have. The way mothers do." She thinks about the baby teeth, how she could have dated those ziplock bags.

"The parrot was like a member of the family," the husband says. "That's what I heard."

"I have to be somewhere," she says, but her husband is already heading back inside to his computer. He has seen something she missed, the mother is sure. He is reporting it to the neighborhood watch, posting on the listserv. "I took pills," she says or doesn't say.

The door to the nondenominational church is locked, so the mother knocks and waits, then sits down on the front stoop, her hand making a brim over her eyes to keep out the four-o'clock sun. She thinks about getting back in her car but has driven here in a Vicodin cloud that now feels thicker instead of lighter. She is waiting for it to pass when the door finally opens behind her. The sound makes the mother jump like she's been shot.

"It's okay," a woman says. Her voice as kind and maternal as taffy. "You don't have to be alone. Come in."

"Are you from the welcome committee?" the mother says.

"All are welcome here," the woman says. She has a mole on her chin that the mother wants to touch. She wonders if it's as soft as the woman's voice or more like a scab. The mother wants to touch the woman's shoulders, maybe rest her head on one of them.

"I've lost my daughter," the mother says. The woman is holding her hands and pulling her up now.

"No wonder you're so light," the woman says. "We've all lost something."

The church is cool, and darker than the mother remembers. The woman hands her a rag. "You can help me dust the chairs," she says. "Many hands."

"I only have two."

"Make light work," the woman says.

The mother does not want to dust the white folding chairs. She could have stayed home if she wanted to dust, but she swipes her rag over the back of row after row in her section. They have divided the church in two. The woman hums something while she dusts, and the mother thinks about humming something, too, but she can't remember any songs. The last time she heard the painful ache of music was right here in this church when someone held her hand, a man who wanted to help her find her daughter.

"Thank you," the woman says, taking her rag from her. "Now let me get you something to eat. When is the last time you ate?"

The kitchen in the church is all stainless steel, but not the new expensive kind popular in remodels. The silver appliances and counters in the church's kitchen are bent and shiny in a way that makes the mother think of dented cans.

"Here we go," the church woman says, staring into the massive refrigerator and pulling out a loaf of bread and large jars of generic peanut butter and grape jelly. She makes two sandwiches. The mother wonders how she'll swallow even one.

She gets out two pink plastic plates from one of the metal cabinets and gives them each a sandwich. "Let's eat together," the woman says. "No one should have to eat alone."

The mother has not had a peanut butter and jelly sandwich in many years, not since her daughter was little. They ate them together, or maybe she ate the sandwich her daughter didn't eat, that her daughter left on the table because food was dull and there was something else to do somewhere else in the house that seemed more urgent or fun or she just wasn't hungry. "Not all children are food driven," the pediatrician had said when the mother told him how picky she was, the long list of foods she shunned, the few she suffered through.

The woman sits down across from the mother at the long table in the kitchen and reaches across the table to take the mother's hands. "We are thankful for Your bounty," the woman says and lets go.

Now that they have held hands, the mother wonders for a second if she could reach out and touch the woman's mole, but doesn't. "I would like to," she says, letting the sentence end there.

"It can take a while," the woman says. "Don't be hard on yourself. We all find Him in our own way."

The woman talks with food in her mouth.

Swallow first, the mother wants to say. *Chew with your mouth closed.* "Swallow your words," the mother says instead.

The woman smiles at her with a full mouth as if the mother has said something kind, as if she is a good person, not a woman who has driven away her own daughter, not a woman who has driven to this church stoned on decades-old narcotics.

"I'm not who you think I am," the mother says.

"I myself," the woman says. "There but for the grace. Aren't you hungry? You look so hungry. You're very thin."

The mother takes a small bite of her sandwich, chews. She feels something stick to the peanut butter and tries to keep chewing. It is her daughter's baby tooth or a piece of a pill next to her gum. Maybe she was wrong. Maybe it didn't all dissolve. Or maybe she is swallowing her own teeth now. Maybe next she will swallow her tongue. She feels something go down. The woman hands her a glass of tap water, and the mother swallows and swallows. She has never been this thirsty.

"There," the woman says.

"Where?" the mother tries to say, but she cannot speak, swallowing and swallowing.

"There," the woman sing-songs. "There you go."

Offering

When my sister, Marla, comes to visit, we decide to take a hike to the Hollywood sign. She lived here two decades ago when we were both in our early twenties. We were even roommates for a year, sharing a sun-filled bedroom with splintery wood floors on the second level of a pink fourplex in not-quite Silverlake. When Marla decided to move to the Valley to be closer to the industry, specifically closer to the semi-abandoned warehouse buildings where she often auditioned, I edged closer to the west side.

You might remember her as the pretty but annoying neighbor on any number of short-lived television sitcoms, the kind of shows they don't make anymore. She was the one who knocked at the door, carrying a lemon cake or oatmeal cookies or a peach pie to welcome the new neighbors. And then it turned out the cake tasted like dandruff or the cookies crumbled like sawdust or the pie was store bought and stale, or she dropped it, the jelled peaches spreading like mold on the newly installed carpet.

She even had a few movie roles, mostly doing *background work* as she was careful to call it. She was quick to remind you if you met her at a party that there was nothing extra about any of it.

My sister used to be the kind of elegantly undernourished girl who could show up late at a party sulking and leave early with the sexiest guy there. I watched Marla do this so many times I stopped going out with her, even with the promise of free alcohol and food. Instead, I stuck a frozen Lean Cuisine in the microwave and stayed home and studied for the bar exam. Which is not easy to pass, by the way, in California.

Now my sister lives in the desert with her husband, Don. He had a few decent roles as a drugged-out house painter and an empathetic bartender, but he found his real niche playing cowboys in movies. Sometimes he still does, filming outside of

Lone Pine or in the scrubs of Joshua Tree. Mostly, he's retired now even though he's not yet fifty. If you ran into him in line at Ralphs or El Pollo Loco, you'd recognize his profile and wonder where you'd seen him.

My sister met him at one of the parties after I stopped going with her. She went home with him and in the morning walked into our apartment, put on a new pot of coffee and ran a shower as if her life hadn't changed one bit. He hounded her for weeks after that until she let him take her out on a real date. He picked her up on his motorcycle, but he may as well have been riding a quarter horse to our Silverlake-adjacent fourplex. I'm not the easily swayed type, but I'd be lying if I didn't say I felt something buckle inside of me when he walked up our stairwell with a hand gripped tight around a bunch of white daisies.

They live in a trailer on the edge of a lot where they're building their dream home. I haven't been out there for months, but last Christmas when I visited, the house was still mostly just poured cement, a few two-by-fours poking out. Don drew the rooms in chalk for me, and I walked through them as reverently as possible while he described the layout. I tried not to watch him move. His shoulders, his back, all of it impossible. "The atrium will be two floors high," he said, looking up at a flat blue sky.

Now I follow my sister up a hill. We'd originally parked in Beachwood Canyon, only to find that trail closed behind a locked iron gate, and had to compete for parking in Griffith Park to hike a longer, more populated trail. Star Waggons had taken over a chunk of the lots. Of course they had. Running into filming was unavoidable here.

My sister was furious that I didn't know the Hollyridge trail was closed. "Jesus, it's been closed almost two years," she said more than once as we drove away, and she typed furiously into her phone, figuring out where we should go. "You're the one who lives here. You should have known."

"It's not like I go hiking every day," I said. "I do have a job."

"Whatever," she said.

My job as an entertainment lawyer is of little interest to Marla now that she's left the industry. I have plenty of gossip, some even about A-listers, but I'm not allowed to share it. Attorney/client privilege. Still, I used to tell Marla. I wouldn't give her names, just a first initial, and sometimes I even made that up, but we would open a bottle of something pricey, and if Don was there, I was suddenly the one who commanded the attention, not my glamorous little sister. Now I may as well work at Rite Aid as far as Marla's concerned.

We're halfway up the trail, and she's still angry. Marla's stomping on rocks, and I'm doing my best to keep up. She's no longer razor thin. Her butt is pushing out against her yoga pants, and I can see the seam pulling open at the middle. Her hair is in a high ponytail. Despite the weight gain, the truth is, she looks more like an irritated curvy teenager than the forty-two-year-old she is. My own hair is short and thin. The last stylist I saw highlighted it strategically and cut it in layers that were supposed to make it look fuller, but instead it looks wilted, with random swatches of color as if I were deciding on wall paint for my kitchen.

I feel the top of my head burning. Driving here and parking took another forty-five minutes, and that translated into ten more degrees. Marla was so quick to get out of the car and start hiking, I left my hat and sunglasses behind trying to keep up with her, and now I try to keep my gaze low as if that will protect me from sunburn.

When Marla stops, I think it's because she's finally decided to wait for me. Maybe she's not mad anymore, or she wants to talk. I still don't know why she's visiting me. All she said was that she wanted to go hiking, and I took a Friday off to give us a long weekend together. Maybe we'd go to the beach on Saturday, I thought, the farmers' market on Sunday. I'd treat her like company instead of competition. Weren't we too old to compare lives?

I heard my phone beeping in my back pocket as we started out up the trail, but it's silent now, not because my work has stopped trying to get in touch with me despite my day off, but because no one has reception up here. The silence is more startling to me than the constant pings.

We are all stopped, not just Marla and me. A group of three girls wearing running shorts and orange Pepperdine tee shirts cut off at their midriffs have their phones out and are taking photos of something ahead of them. "I think that's him," one of them says.

"Fuck yes!" another says.

A small crowd of hikers has formed now, tourists with fancy folding hiking sticks, two men walking their dogs on tight leashes. I assume the men are partners because of their matching dogs, a large, frightening breed people are always calling intelligent. German shepherds maybe. I am not an animal person. I once took care of a colleague's cat for the weekend when I was new at my firm and afraid of saying no and dry-heaved every time I scooped out the kitty litter.

Temporary metal fences are blocking the rest of the trail. "Oh, Jesus Christ. Now what," Marla says, but she's looking too.

I listen to the Pepperdine girls talking and find out they've come up here to watch a scene from a movie being filmed, hoping to catch a glimpse of its star. They have been doing detective work online, tracking this down, apparently arguing about the exact location. One of them says, "See, I told you I was right."

We don't represent him, but I've heard the actor's name muttered in our office. Someone is after him, has been talking to his manager. He's only twenty-two, but he's big, already being compared to Tom Cruise, Brad Pitt and Leonardo DiCaprio.

He is hiking up the trail in front of us, the one we're not allowed on, bundled up in a down jacket despite the heat, a rifle slung over his shoulder, walking toward a camera and a huge, mop-like mic.

"He's so hot," one of the Pepperdine girls says.

"OMG," another one adds.

"He can shoot me anytime," the third one says.

They are all blond and slim and anywhere but here, where they look like nearly everyone else, they might be mistaken for budding movie stars themselves.

"Do you have any idea who I am?" Marla says to them.

"Should we?" one of them says, turning away from the filming and wrinkling up her freckled nose in a way her boyfriend probably finds adorable.

Marla stares at her for so long, I feel my heart start to pound. She is capable, my sister, of saying almost anything. "Not really," Marla says. "Come on, Colleen. Let's get out of here."

Walking down the hill, Marla is slower, and I have to measure my own stride to her pace. "It was only a matter of time," she says.

"What was?" I say.

"Come on. Everyone knew it was only a matter of time."

And suddenly I do know. Don. I am not proud of my reaction. But here it is: I think, why didn't I sleep with him if he was going to cheat on my sister anyway? It may just as well have been me.

"A fucking hostess at some scumball restaurant in Twentynine Palms."

"Oh, I'm sorry, Marla," I say, and now that I've gotten ahold of myself, I am.

"Maybe I'll move back in with you," she says. "Just like the old days. Remember how much fun we had?"

I'm searching for an answer that doesn't come when we hear the gunshot. Our hero has been shot at while hiking, or maybe he's shot someone. Or shot at a bird or a deer or a rattlesnake. Yes, probably a rattlesnake. They wouldn't even have to import one—these hills are filled with them—but I'm sure they did.

One of the dogs that had been held so tightly on its leash is off and running past us, its leash dragging behind it. I push Marla out of the way. We are in the scrub on the side of the trail when the dog's owner comes running after him. "Shit!" he is screaming. "Get back here, Henry."

Marla starts laughing first, and then I'm laughing, too. "That poor dog," I say. "That poor man. We're being mean."

"You were never mean," Marla says. "I'm the mean one."

I think about telling Marla something mean about myself, how sometimes I go home with men the way she used to. I meet them at bars or online. I don't want anything that lasts. I like my apartment with its clean surfaces and can't imagine what a man's discarded socks and emptied pockets would add to my life. But I don't tell Marla any of this. I also don't tell her about the mammogram I had three years ago that required *further monitoring* and now how I have to schedule special appointments every year where the woman who checks me in smiles with practiced pity. We haven't been that kind of sisters, and it seems too late to become that now.

Our parents, who live in Danville, a Bay Area suburb people afraid of San Francisco move to when they have children, have stopped hinting about grandchildren. We're too old now. I think about how at least Marla is married and I'm a lawyer, how our parents have that. But maybe Marla will be divorced, and they'll just have the part about me to remind themselves they didn't fail and have something to talk about at dinner parties. But instead of feeling victorious, I just feel sad.

Marla and I walk together back down the trail the rest of the way without talking, my phone now beeping again in my back pocket. I don't have to tell Marla that she can't live with me, despite my spare bedroom with the queen bed with the good mattress. All I have to do is pretend she didn't ask.

"Maybe you two can work it out," I say.

"I doubt it," she says. "Come on," Marla pulls me over to a Star Waggon where they have set out a buffet of food, salads and salami and olives and cheese and fruit, for the crew and cast. "Just play along," she says. "Don't say anything."

Marla smiles her still dazzling smile at a man lining up water bottles, and we grab thick plastic plates and load them up. Spilled food from our plates trails behind us as we navigate through cars back to ours.

When we hear the brakes squeal in the road at the far end of the parking lot, Marla drops her plate and grips the top of my arm so tightly, she makes a bruise that will last for days after she drives back to her trailer in the desert. We hear the barks and screams and don't have to see anything to know the man whose dog escaped is bent over in the road next to the parking lot, crying.

"I can't look," she says.

"Let's not," I say.

"We should help," Marla says.

"What could we do," I say, a statement, not a question.

Despite myself, I turn and look in the direction where the dog has been hit. I see the man carrying it now in a blanket someone must have given him. He is walking through the parking lot, holding the covered dog out in front of him like some kind of offering, the other man and his dog taut on his leash following behind. I'm not sure, but I think I can hear him crying from here, or maybe it's just a red fox off in the hills somewhere, screaming out in urgent primal longing.

My sister loosens her grip on my arm, and I reach for her hand as if we are eight and six again, instead of the disappointing adult cowards we have become. I used to walk her home from school this way, her child fingers linked through mine.

Shopping for Dad

We are shopping for Dad. We have the whole family to choose from, but we go for Dad. We know the story. Everyone wants the girl with her cloying requests for dolls and crayons. And the loud kiss-ups want to impress the teacher with the skateboard for the boy. Look how generous I am, they shout! Still in the box. And Mom with her makeup kit has her do-good followers. But who will take Dad if not us?

Our math teacher asked who amongst us could find it in our hearts to help a family in need before the holidays? She passed around the list, and we checked off Dad's name. "We've got Dad's sweater," we told her after class. "You can check that one off the list."

"You already did," she said.

We scour the mall looking for Dad's sweater. We don't know what will go with his skin tones, what his skin tones are, but we do our best. We imagine what our art teacher calls "olive." Dad wants a large. But we worry he's overestimated. After all, he listed his pants size as 34. We picture Dad in his huge sweater that clashes with his skin, his hair. His narrow waist in there somewhere. *Oh, Dad*, we think. *Let down again.*

In each store, we gravitate toward the sales racks in the back as if shopping for our own disappointing fathers with their dandruff flakes and sagging bellies, but then remember and pull on each other's belt loops until we are back in the unfamiliar front of the store.

"Full price," we tell each other. "This is Dad we're talking about here." But each sweater is wrong for Dad. The wool may make him itch. The cotton seems not quite a sweater at all. Where will he find the money to dry-clean the cashmere?

We take a break from shopping for Dad and shop for ourselves. We excel at shoplifting. But today we try to remember our mission, to F-O-C-U-S, as our math teacher says, writing the letters out on the dry-erase board in thick black lines she'll later smear down her sleeve. We push each other into a rack of earrings, and while we bend over to pick them up, we each pocket only one shiny pair.

We decide on this silently.

Later on, in the food court, dipping our soft pretzels into each other's tubs of icing, we discover we've both gone for hoops. We're spooky this way.

We hold them up to each other's ears, pretending we're mirrors. Although we both know the truth.

Which one of us has the fat lobes.

Who amongst us is prettier.

"Let's get back to Dad," we say.

"F-O-C-U-S."

We clean up our table, dump the leftover stubs of our pretzels in the garbage can. We may be thieves, but we're neat. After years of bussing our cafeteria trays, we can't help ourselves.

We pass a group of boys, the kind who stick french fries up their noses and sneeze them out across the table at each other. "I'd like some of that," they say. "Come sit on my lap, and we'll talk about whatever pops up."

"Dream on, losers," we say. They're not from our school. What do we care? We writhe past them in our tight low jeans in slow motion like we're in a music video. Hot and mean.

"Oh, baby, you're killing us," they say.

We are capable of worse.

We excel at making eighth-grade boys squirm. We're such a distraction we bring down the entire grade curve in our history class. Sometimes we make out with boys, let them press our bodies flat against the gymnasium wall after a dance, but mostly we babysit.

We prefer them before they can talk. Real babies. But we don't say no when the parents call us to watch the older ones.

The bed-wetters. The whiners. The five-year-old girls who brush our hair for hours with tiny Barbie accessories. We save all the money. For the right moment. This is one of those moments. Shopping for Dad's sweater.

In a full-price rack we find a large, depressing pumpkin-colored sweater. Exhausted with indecision, we can't help ourselves. Who amongst us could? *Dad will understand*, we think, getting the thing boxed up, laying out our cash.

We wait with Dad's sweater for the bus. We're in the right spot at the right time, and still we have to wait. We strike bored poses, tugging our pants lower while we pretend to pull them up. We excel at waiting.

Dad would be here on time, we think.

The sun beats down on top of our heads.

We feel our shoulders freckle and burn.

Juggling

Tyler is on the phone talking to his therapist, Frank, because it's ten-thirty on Friday night and he has nothing better to do. The idea is to make things sound interesting, so Frank stays on the line. Outside a car door slams, and Tyler walks, still talking on the phone, over to the front window and cracks open the blinds. The phone is black and slim, almost flat. It reminds Tyler of the phone inside Agent Smart's shoe on the old TV show he watches late at night. It has that kind of feel in his hand. He's set it so it doesn't ring. It beeps like a computer issuing a warning. His last phone felt hollow. He set it to sound like an alarm clock.

"I have this feeling," Tyler says, watching a woman get out of her car and walk not to his house, but to the nearly identical one next door, "that the world has turned against me."

"You've had that feeling before, and things improved," Frank says.

"You're just like all of them. You think I'm handling things just fine." There's no other action out there. Tyler pulls the blinds shut and paces around looking for something, anything in this house worthy of his attention.

"Is your mother there?" Frank says.

"Why? Did you want to talk to her? A conference call. You don't think I have enough to say, is that it?"

"Here's what I want you to do," Frank says. "I want you to cool out, take a walk, smoke a joint, whatever. I want you to call me tomorrow afternoon and tell me how you did, if the world's looking up."

"Have fun tonight. Life's a party, Frank," Tyler says. "Thanks for the sex tips." Tyler turns the phone off and tries to turn it back on to make another call, but the battery is dead. He pushes the little buttons in above the numbers, and still there is nothing. Tyler looks deep into the phone resting belly-up in his hand, and for the first time all day, he relaxes.

Tyler's mother, Laura, is out with her boyfriend, Reese. She is always out with Reese, or she is at work at Floral Designs, where she arranges flowers and takes antihistamines. It's just like Laura, Tyler thinks, to take a job that makes her sick. She believes all allergies and most illnesses are psychosomatic. She believes she will overcome her weaknesses when she overcomes her allergies. Laura makes Tyler laugh.

It seems to Tyler that most women are wrong about the world. They spend all of their time worrying about the wrong things. Just tonight, Sara stood him up because she's waiting for her cat to have kittens. She's building a kind of nest for the cat in a laundry basket, pulling the yarn out of old sweaters. She didn't even invite him to come over and help, as if this nest-making would take all night.

Tyler walks outside and looks at his cars parked in the driveway. He has two cars, a Mustang and a Chevy Nova, good old solid cars, but neither of them is running at the moment. In the Mustang he has installed an old CD player. At least that's running. He gets into the car and listens to Jimi Hendrix, a man who, like Janis Joplin, knew when he was burnt out and it was time to die.

Tyler once had a girlfriend who looked like Janis. She wore her hair long and wild with a tiny braid that fell by her face. Her name was Calli, and listening to Jimi in his Mustang, Tyler remembers something she used to do to his back, how her fingers made him curl up like an inchworm. She didn't last. None of his girlfriends last. When Tyler gets this car running, he's going to install a car phone. He'll call Calli as he's driving down to the Keys, and he'll say to her, guess who this is, guess where I'm heading?

In the glove compartment, Tyler finds a pair of pliers and a can of tennis balls. He brings the tennis balls inside with him. In his room, he juggles first two and then three. He used to be a good tennis player, and now he's a good juggler. When the balls leave his hand he knows where each one of them is going, at exactly which instant they will turn in the air. His mother, Laura, cannot stand it when he juggles, the ease of his skill. She would like to know why he cannot devote this kind of concentration to his schoolwork, why he cannot juggle the numbers in his Algebra class, the sentences in his English papers. What she doesn't understand is that juggling takes no concentration at all for Tyler, that the balls move with their own light energy.

When Laura complains about Tyler's juggling, Reese says, "Leave the boy alone for once, Laura," and bounces his car keys in his hand. Tyler gives Reese the creeps, and Tyler knows and enjoys this. "How about those Giants?" Tyler says to Reese any time of the year. "You want to talk a little football?" Reese coaches at Tyler's high school. Tyler has heard him tell Laura that it wouldn't hurt to get that son of hers in a uniform, that he might put those big shoulders to some use.

Tyler goes into the bathroom and washes his hands, which have the dusty smell of tennis balls on them. He combs his hair in the bathroom mirror, so it covers the thin scar on his forehead. The scar is the result of a tricycle accident he had when he was three and has begun to bother Tyler only recently. He is concerned that it looks like a wrinkle, that it makes him look older than he is. He is only seventeen, younger than Jim Morrison was when he wrote his first song.

The phone is charged again. Tyler calls Sara back to see if she's changed her mind and wants to come get him so they can go out, but nobody answers. He sends her a text message. This is just like a woman to fuck you over. Tyler walks around the house with the phone, kicking at the furniture. The truth is that he only tried to kill Laura once, and that he really didn't try to kill her. He threw the kitchen knife at the wall next to her over a year ago, and she had gone screaming out into the street. That was before she started going out with Reese, after Tyler's father, Calvin, moved out of their house in Virginia to live with Julia in Silver

Spring. He took his things with him in a plastic garbage bag and handed Tyler his new address on a piece of paper. "I guess we all saw this coming for a while," is what Calvin said to him.

Tyler had seen nothing coming. He had been fifteen years old and considering his options, whether to become a chemist, whether to sign up for tennis camp again that summer. In Frank's office, Tyler has demonstrated for him how he threw the knife. He aimed the air gathered between his thumb and finger at Frank's heart and got himself a psychologist for life. "I want you to know that your mother and father agree on this issue," Frank told him. "You can call me anytime you want."

Now Tyler is worried. Frank seems to be losing interest. It is taking him longer and longer to return Tyler's calls. Recently at Frank's office, Tyler has seen Frank gazing out his window, hardly listening at all.

Tyler falls down on the bed in Laura's room. He rolls from the side of the bed that was his father's to his mother's side. Sometimes Reese sleeps here now. Late at night, Tyler hears Laura wheezing and Reese running water for her to take with her pills. Her wheezing got worse after Calvin left, and she took the job at the florist. In the morning she smiles at Tyler over her newspaper, and Tyler hears the whistle in her throat.

Frank says of all the players involved, why should Laura be the one Tyler blames? He says Tyler has to learn to look inside himself for answers and not to the outside world for fault. At Julia's house, Tyler's father made herb tea and asked Tyler to have a seat. "Julia's at her aerobics class," Calvin said, "otherwise she would be happy to meet you." Tyler had never seen his father drink anything warm. In the mornings he drank orange juice but never coffee. At night ice floated in his drinks. "I guess in a couple of years you'll be off at college," Calvin said, Tyler's knife suspended in the air between them, dangerous and silent.

Since then he has met Julia several times. He's sat on one side of her, his father on the other, at foreign movies in D.C.,

Julia's small, manicured hands folded neatly in her lap. Whenever Tyler is around her, all he can think about is his father and Julia doing it, who gets on top, what kind of noise his father makes when he comes. But Tyler is very polite nonetheless, always keeps the conversation light, careful to give his father no reason for disappearing from his life completely.

Tyler gets out of his mother's bed and walks into the living room, over to the window, and cracks open the blinds. There is never anything going on in this neighborhood. When Laura and Reese get back, Tyler is going to tease Reese about his butch haircut. As soon as he gets his Mustang going again, he's going to get out of here. In the kitchen, he takes two and then three knives out of the heavy knife block. He holds the knives in one hand, their wooden handles solid and warm, and closes his eyes. He is juggling.

Freshman

In college, a girl named Jade sells sugar cube acid door-to-door. If you were a lesbian and in love with her, she would certainly reject you. Instead, she barely notices you as she slips your money into a fold of her skirts. Over the next weeks, you'll notice that pockets are sewn into all of her clothes in mysterious places.

After arriving by bus from Delaware to find a group of hugging students singing "Love the One You're With" on the quad outside your dorm, you're afraid to leave your room. It seems that everyone but you knew to get here early for the optional summer camping trip, that there was nothing truly optional about this trip at all. When you look outside your window, you're stunned by how happy everyone seems in their frisbee-tossing and dandelion-chain-making groups.

Although the acid doesn't help you leave your room, it does make your decision to stay put seem more sensible. By sucking down lemon drops instead of water when you're thirsty, you're able to plan trips down the hall only when the bathroom's empty, usually in the middle of the day when nearly everyone's in class and in the middle of the night, when they're asleep. The bathroom, with its row of gleaming showers, is much bigger than your tiny dorm room, and even without the acid, you reason, it would take a moment to adjust to such shiny vastness. You pick a toilet cubicle and hurry while you're still alone. Back in your room, the walls shimmer, your books unfold their pages and read to you, all of the usual reassuring psychedelic tricks.

You are eighteen and in your first week of college and your boyfriend, Chris, is in Brazil to hunt down the money his mother left for him and his drunk father squirreled away in a foreign bank account. You are aggressively faithful to Chris in a way that is only possible at eighteen when your brother is in a hippie boarding/reform school in Colorado and your parents have finally left each other for other people. You're faithful in the drooling stray dog sort of way, grateful that anyone has bothered to pat your mangy, pathetic head. It doesn't occur to you that Chris may feel differently, that you slip as easily in and out of his consciousness as the name of a diner in New Jersey where he used to order a very decent skirt steak.

You make friends with a girl you don't like named Diane. She seems betrayed to find herself in this hippie no-grade college. It's as if she's registered for secretarial classes and her application was intercepted by a band of roving Deadheads. She doesn't do drugs, but she does smoke, and together you smoke in her room after dinner while Diane leans into a lighted vanity mirror and pops invisible forehead zits and talks about her boyfriend on Long Island. Diane is small and blond and pretty in a way that you already recognize as the kind of pretty that may get you into a concert for free but probably won't get you backstage to party with the band. You have brown hair that is neither straight nor curly and is always in some indefinite stage of growing out or coming in. You are way too unsure of your own appearance to look into a mirror in front of anyone else and pop an actual zit, which you have. Still, you have this one thing in common: your missing boyfriends.

You have already had a string of friends like Diane and will have a string more, girls with whom you share one single problem—bad singing voices, pimples that sprout up on your back, missing boyfriends—and pretend this is the same thing as friendship. These are girls that talk and talk and don't notice whether you respond or not. Girls like radios. Girls that speak one foreign language badly and loudly and with way too much confidence, as if they learned to speak it, no matter how solidly middle class they are, by ordering around their parents' household help.

You're finally so lonely from alternating evenings listening to Diane and dropping acid alone in your dorm room that you vow to make a new friend. You begin in your dorm, finally venturing out of your room to walk down the hallway to the bathroom at an hour when other people might still be awake. You smile in the one open door you find, where a girl sits on her bed, an upside-down American flag on the wall above her, underlining a textbook, earphones plugged in. You hear giggling behind another door, the grunts of sex behind the next, Kurt Cobain's plaintive voice wailing out behind the last.

You give up on the new friend idea and write to your boyfriend in Brazil, who's already graduated from a better college than this one. Because it is more romantic than email, you write long letters by hand with leaky pens. You pretend to understand Kant and Plato and Camus after making it to two philosophy classes during which the professor sat barefoot and cross-legged on the floor, his Birkenstocks next to him like a sleeping cat, and read aloud to the class, closing his book after passages that seemed somehow particularly pointed to him and sighing out at the class knowingly. Once, you found yourself sitting across from him in the dim light of the co-ed sauna, and he was staring off at this invisible point, his white towel draped over his lap.

You go to enough of all of your classes not to call attention to yourself. In this way, you remain invisible and dumb and, each day, more over your head with doubt. In the cafeteria, you stand several times in the buffet line each night, where you take refills on sweet-and-sour tofu, tempeh burgers, hunks of battered deep-fried cauliflower. Sometimes you sit with Diane. Sometimes you sit with your dorm mates. The girl with the upside-down flag and the highlighter pen is named Jan. She has long black hair with two inches of split ends. She has blue eyes and a nose spotted with freckles and is desperately behind in all of her classes, despite all the underlining. She is nice to you. She is nice to everyone, but who cares at this point if she's not particular. You're just grateful when she smiles at you and pats an empty seat next to her.

Your other dorm mates are more problematic. Ryan is graduating in May but still living in his freshman room instead of one of the coveted campus apartments where most older students live. He has so intricately wired his room, he can barely manage to leave it. He's the only person you know who may miss more classes than you do. If you go into his room high and happen to touch the wrong light switch, Ryan screams and his computer flashes neon bars of color; his television buzzes with purple static, and two Philip Glass cuts play at once, one forward and one backward.

Your other dorm mates that occasionally sit with your group are Evan and Tony. Evan's father is a famous psychotherapist that you've never heard of but know that you should have. Evan is dark and brooding and focuses on his food as if it might be poisoned. Tony is six foot six and a DJ for a blues radio station. He looks thirty, and it's unclear to you whether he's a student or not. There's always music in his head. He taps his spoon on the table while he chews each bite.

You buy parachute pants with a drawstring waist and cry the first time you catch sight of yourself in them, reflected in a thrift store window. You have never been fat before and didn't realize this was a possibility. You stuff all of your clothes that no longer fit you under your bed and buy waistless dresses from Guatemala, tiny mirrors sewn into the fabric.

You decide that getting involved in politics might make you forget how fat and lonely you've become. After attending one meeting during which thirty students use the better part of an hour to order a pizza by consensus instead of voting on the toppings, you climb into someone's bumper-sticker-plastered minivan and drive to a nuclear power plant to protest its existence. You camp in the woods, get hit with billy clubs and spend the better part of one night trying to keep a man named Storm from feeling you up when you are all supposed to be sharing sleeping bags, so you don't get hypothermia. You become constipated from living on dry granola and apple juice for three days and miss even more classes. When you get back to your dorm, you fall asleep for twenty hours, and when you wake up, your boyfriend is back, pounding on your door.

Chris eyes you suspiciously. "You look different," he says, and, in that instant, you realize you have been waiting for the wrong person. You take him in anyway, despite the fact that for one moment of alarming lucidity you know you are making the kind of monumental mistake that you will spend the next four years trying to justify and the following four trying to get over. In an effort to impress him with your intellectuality, you attend a few more classes than usual while he rolls joints in your dorm room and yells in Portuguese on his cell phone to banks in Rio. Since he's not supposed to be here, you sneak him home what you can for dinner, usually salami and cheese and cherry tomatoes funneled deep into the cone of your double chocolate ice cream.

In summer, everyone clears out of the dorms except Evan, who manages to get a phony job on campus, so he doesn't have to leave his room, and most of the college students leave town. It feels like a huge emptying out, like your childhood in reverse, when summer people came screeching into your tiny Delaware beach town in wood-framed station wagons, sticky kids whining in the backseat. Chris and you stay and move into the one slum in the upscale college town you are able to find, a ground-floor apartment in a building that, with its concave front porches and missing asbestos shingles, looks not only deserted but scheduled for demolition.

But it isn't deserted. You have five sets of neighbors, including a beautiful boy above your apartment. He dropped out of college five years before, works as a carpenter and dates a woman who always looks startled and fresh, as if she's just stepped out of a shower and has been caught naked. This is a woman you hate on principle and with pure envy. Above them are three gay men who serve you red zinger iced tea on their fire escape balcony whenever you lock yourself out, which turns out to be fairly often. They have a snake they keep in a fish tank in the living room. The snake has a tendency to crawl out and hide in the couch pillows, so you avoid their invitations to come in and pretend to enjoy nonexistent summer breezes on their balcony until Chris gets home from job hunting and lets you back in.

They aren't the only snake people. On the second floor on the other side of the building, a huge man and tiny woman keep snakes and rats and lizards and let their dishes pile up until they fall over and shatter on the floor. They are rumored to be geniuses, AWOL from a PhD program in Physics at U. Mass. Above and below them are the transient neighbors, confusing combinations of mothers and sons and boyfriends with motorcycles and daughters with tube tops and lots of late-night arguments and an occasional visit by the police, which sends the rest of you flushing everything illegal you can remember you have down the toilets and clogging your already eternally jammed-up plumbing system.

You get a job at the Greek diner across the street, where you're paid odd amounts of cash every two or three weeks and are mistaken for one of the boss's rebellious daughters so often you stop correcting people. Instead, you sit at the table with the boss's wife, Evelyn, during slow times and smoke Pall Malls while her daughters sneak out back to smoke their own cigarettes. You easily assume your new identity, Greek and put upon and just plain damn tired.

Meanwhile, Chris finds the most unlikely job either one of you can imagine for him. Without even bothering to fake empathy, he becomes a social worker for an agency that mistakes his liberal arts degree for a degree in humanity. You celebrate by having wild, unprotected sex, and immediately become pregnant.

You spend the rest of the summer crying and arguing with Chris and making and canceling clinic appointments and taking home stray kittens and stuffing pillows under your Guatemalan dresses and smoking Pall Malls with Evelyn and feeling old and sad and wise and inconsolable. One day, you stay in bed crying so long that your body finally turns itself inside out like a coat lining and you start bleeding. Soon, the whole thing is over—you will always be better at making decisions you never really have to make—but at a bright, shiny clinic, a nurse holds your hand and a doctor scrapes you out for good measure anyway.

In the recovery room, you lie on a cot in the warm socks you remembered to pack, and a kind, moon-faced volunteer feeds you juice and cookies while Chris reads to you from a waiting room magazine. And you realize that, in many ways, this is the sweetest moment of your first year away at college, and you vow right then to make some changes during your sophomore year.

How This Works

When the mother gets home from the church, she boils water to make tea and slides open a kitchen drawer to find a teaspoon to stir in honey. But most of the teaspoons have disappeared. There is only one in the slot where eight should be nested in a thick pile. The single spoon left there has been ravaged in the garbage disposal, the oval mouth of it chewed and spit out.

This shouldn't be a surprise to the mother, but she jolts back when she sees the single spoon. Their neighborhood has been plagued by small thefts. A baseball bat left under a squat palm tree gone along with several low-hanging fronds, a collar slipped off the neck of an outdoor cat, tulips cut with the precision of an X-Acto knife blade from a side yard.

And now this.

She will tell her husband about the spoons, and he will be pleased that she noticed. So many little thefts. They must be recorded. He is in charge of the recording and the neighborhood watch. Her husband is so busy he has barely noticed that their nineteen-year-old daughter left their home in the middle of her spring break from college and disappeared, too, deleted from their lives for two months now. She doesn't answer texts or phone calls or emails. The mother has even tried a Facebook message. All of it ignored.

I should have been more patient, the mother thinks. *I shouldn't have made her get out of bed. I should have taken her sadness over that boy more seriously.*

The mother turns the spoon upside down to stir her tea, so the gnawed-up mouth doesn't rip open the tea bag, and the string comes loose from the rim of the cup and loops around the stem.

In truth, she never liked this flatware, would have preferred something plainer than the braided floral design. Something truly flat. She remembers choosing it quickly years ago at a department store before their daughter was born when they were first married, and picking a neighborhood and a house and silverware were equal parts momentous and meaningless. When mostly they just wanted to go back to their bedroom and pull shut the blackout blinds and sink deep into each other's bodies, amazed at their single-minded good luck.

Now, her husband's body is as familiar and tuneless to the mother as a dining room chair, a dishwasher, a potted plant. When she bumps into him, it is by accident, as she does now in the kitchen when he walks in and takes a beer out of the refrigerator.

"The teaspoons," she says.

"I didn't see you there," he says.

"They're gone."

"Time to run the dishwasher maybe," he says.

The mother opens the dishwasher, and she stares at seven teaspoons draped across the cup rack. "Oh," she says. "Of course."

Her husband is carrying a clipboard in one hand, his beer in the other. "Making some notes," he says. "It's important to keep track."

"I was," the mother says, but he has already left the kitchen. He is walking through the house and out the front door. His beer is balancing on his clipboard now, and he is pulling out a pen from behind his ear and walking down the block slowly, shuffling really, as if he might be older than he is, as if he might be his own father, stopping and inching his beer over on the clipboard where it is balanced, so he can write things down. So he can make note.

The mother has joined an online group for parents of missing children, and she logs in and lurks around the edges of the conversations. The children are runaways and drug addicts, and they are running away from home and running away from their aunts' and grandparents' houses where the parents have sent them and living on the streets, and their parents are sick with worry. Some of their children have just disappeared for no discernible reason at all, and these are the parents whose stories the mother reads and avoids reading. *I don't know what I did wrong,* the parents write. *Tell me. What could I have done differently?* The parents are sleepless and sleeping and they are breaking out in rashes and hives and their stomachs are twisted tight. They have developed ulcers and migraines and aches deep in their bones, aches that feel like some new kind of undiagnosed cancer. The parents in the chat group have hair that is thinning and falling out in clumps. Their children will not talk to them because the parents have failed in ways that are too countless to list.

The parents try to list them anyway. I worked too many hours. I was home too much. I didn't let him breathe. I didn't notice how sad she was. I shouldn't have gotten divorced. I am a terrible mother. I was a lousy father. I should never have had children. I should have had more children. Her father was too strict. We should have moved from the suburbs. We should have been more consistent. I never really wanted children. I always wanted to be a mother. That's all I ever wanted. We shouldn't have moved to the suburbs. I shouldn't have made him cut his hair. I shouldn't have made her wear that dress. I should have let her get that piercing. We should have been more flexible. I should have made her stay in Sunday school. I should have volunteered in the classroom more when he was younger. When I could. I should have left her father. I should have pulled her from that school. I shouldn't have gone back to work. Her father was too lenient. I should have made him unlock that bedroom door. I shouldn't have taken off the door. I should have let her lock her door. I thought it could have been worse. I didn't know it was going to get worse.

I thought it was normal for teenagers.

I thought I was normal.

I thought she was normal.

I thought he was normal.

Is it normal to feel this way?

I thought this was normal.

Thanks for making me feel more normal.

Hello, is anyone out there today?

The mother quickly logs off before she is spotted, although she doesn't know if this is possible, how this works. She is new to chat rooms. She is not a joiner. Her phone is beeping on the desk, and she is afraid to look at it. She decides to let it beep a second time, the way it does when you miss a text. She makes a deal with herself that if she waits, maybe it's her daughter texting. Her daughter will say she's sorry. She's been so busy. *Come down and we can have lunch*, her daughter will say. The mother has been mistaken, and this group of disappeared runaways and drug addicts is not her group at all.

But the text is from the lady at the church one town over where the mother helped clean the chairs and had a sandwich in the middle of that very day, sitting across a thick, dented table in the church kitchen. When the woman asked, the mother remembers now, she had typed her name into the woman's phone before she left, and now she reads:

Just checking to see if you made it home safely.

You are not my daughter, the mother types back and then erases. She had taken Vicodin earlier in the day, but the sweet, blurry effects have worn off. *Yes*, she types. *Here I am. Safely home.*

The mother wants to say there is nothing safe about home, that things have gone missing all over the neighborhood. She walks outside to find her husband. Maybe she can help him make notes, she thinks.

But she doesn't see him when she looks down the block. Instead, she sees a little girl pushing a plastic shopping cart back and forth in front of a rental house. There are other rental houses on the block, but people have lived in those for years. This house has a regular turnover, usually young couples who start out with doormats that scream WELCOME TO OUR HOME before the letters all fade to gray. Hanging pots of begonias dry out on the front porch before the renters move on. This time it's a family. Their little girl chalks the sidewalk in front of their house with pink hearts and yellow smiles.

Today the little girl is pushing a plastic shopping cart back and forth in front of the house. When the mother gets closer, she sees the cart is full of baby dolls that once belonged to the mother's daughter. The mother recognizes the matted hair and blurred eyes, the result of her daughter playing with them in the bathtub despite the fact that they were not made for water. The mother remembers leaving them out on the curb at the end of a yard sale last summer before this family moved into the rental house.

The dolls that weren't ruined were purchased for a dollar each by a woman from Leisure World who planned to make clothes for them and give them to the women to rock who missed their own children and grandchildren. *You'd be surprised what comfort a doll can bring,* the woman had said, stroking a doll's dark hair.

Seeing her daughter's ruined baby dolls being pushed in the plastic shopping cart brings the mother no comfort. "Where did you get those?" she asks the little girl.

"They're my babies," the little girl says.

"No, they're not," the mother says.

The little girl's eyes have welled up and she is grabbing the dolls from the cart and hugging them, but they are tumbling to the ground.

"I'm sorry," the mother says as the front door of the house opens. "We were just chatting," the mother says to the woman who glares at her. "I live down the block." The mother points in the wrong direction and walks that way with purpose.

She walks all the way around the block and sneaks back into her own house. Her husband is standing in the entranceway when she walks in. He is holding up her keys.

"You left the door unlocked," he says.

"I'm sorry," she says. She looks around for his clipboard and finds it on the stairs. The paper clipped onto the board is full of house numbers, check marks and asterisks, her husband's empty beer can tilted over on its side on top of it.

"I was saying hi to the new neighbors," the mother says.

"It's important to keep track," he says.

"The ones with the little girl. I was just out for a minute."

"That's how it happens," he says. "That's how fast."

Illegal Baker

After my husband is attacked by the dog, all the neighbors come by to see us. We're still new on the block, and I don't know any of them yet, not even by face. It turns out we bought our first house on a bitter little street, full of lawsuits and recriminations. In truth, we never looked down this way before we moved in. We're the corner house facing the good block. On the good block we signed on for, no one who actually lives there is home during the day. Nannies push Swedish strollers past well-trimmed lawns that are lined with lavender and night-blooming jasmine. UPS trucks glide to smooth stops. A sleek black cat sleeps, undisturbed, on the pavement.

On the bitter little block it turns out we actually live on, way too many people are home during normal work hours. It's hard to tell the owners from the renters. A huge woman brings her garbage out to the curb, wearing a string bikini. A house with billowing blue plastic covering its roof goes up for sale, listed with a company I never once heard of, and no one comes to look at it.

I know all this because I'm home baking. I'm an illegal baker, but people depend on me. I personally supply a popular coffeehouse in Long Beach with enough overpriced desserts to keep their customers sugar buzzing all week long. Nevertheless, for obvious reasons, *student* is what I listed on our loan forms.

My husband is never home when our neighbors come by to ask after his damaged hand. When Vikkii, a realtor who lives three houses down, hands me her business card (no c, two k's, three i's), takes off her fur-trimmed jacket and settles a little too comfortably into our living room couch at three p.m., the house smells like gingerbread. She looks around, suspicious, when I tell her I don't have children. "We're thinking about it, though," I add.

I can see I'm going to have to offer her a gingerbread cookie. In fact, to get her to leave I'll probably end up sending her home with a plate full and will fall behind on my orders again, the same way I did yesterday when I sent home ten lemon bars with my next-door neighbor, a long-faced man who lives alone in a bungalow, a house, he mumbled after I asked him if he owned it, that he inherited.

Although we bought our house, I ended up feeling an uncomfortable empathy with my neighbor, as if we, too, weren't real homeowners since we had inherited our down payment. Jeff's grandmother doled out her money so fairly in her will that instead of feeling equally loved, each of the cousins ended up feeling equally slighted at not being her favorite. To make up for it, they spent their money in grand pouty gestures. One of the cousins sent us oversized postcards from Marrakesh and Aruba, his inky fingerprints substituting for words. Another had her yellow teeth capped and posed decadently with boas and cigarette holders for Glamour Shots and then sent us a calendar featuring her in a different pose each month. It was Jeff's idea that we do something practical with our portion of the money, which turned out to be just enough for a 5 percent down payment.

"Do you?" I say. "Have any kids, that is."

Vikkii shakes her head. "I'm a bird person myself."

If I were a better neighbor, I would ask her what kind. Instead I excuse myself and take the gingerbread cookies out of the oven while they're still soft. "I'd sue their righteous little butts off if I were you," Vikkii shouts in to me. I bring in a plate of warm cookies and subtract my commission with each bite she takes.

At California Coffee, Jesus lets me in the back door. We're both illegal, but the worst thing that would happen to me if I were found out is I'd have to get a real job. Still, until we bought the house, Jesus treated me like we were comrades, supplying me with free samples of all the Hispanic Avon-like products he helps his wife sell. Now, he calls me Princesa and fakes a little bow when he sees me. When I kiss him hello, I smell Aqua Velva Aftershave.

"How've you been, Jesus?" I ask, pronouncing his name with a hard "J" to get a smile out of him.

"Missing you, Princesa, missing you."

The truth is I'm not above mixing up cooking with sex, but it's not Jesus I'm interested in. My object of lust, my own husband, California Coffee's cook, barely looks up long enough to snicker from his corner of the kitchen where, with his good hand, he chops onions as thin as parchment paper. This is how he is at work, Mr. Concentration. Here's my plan now that we're homeowners: Let's get another loan and start a business. But Jeff says there's not enough security in that. *Take a risk*, is what I think.

I put the gingerbread on the counter, and Jesus hands me my envelope. "Burn a tray again?" he asks. "Better turn off those soaps, Princesa, while you're working."

That night, Jeff and I sit outside on the brick patio, drinking the fruity champagne that our realtor gave us at closing. We don't own any outdoor furniture yet, so we sit on the damp mossy bricks where the hot tub used to be. We thought it came with the house, but when we moved in, it was gone. Our realtor said we should have specified we wanted it, that anything that wasn't bolted down otherwise didn't convey.

"Look, I'm soaking my sore hand," Jeff says, stretching his fingers out in front of him. He's made a splint out of a cereal box top, wrapped electrical tape all around the cotton pads. Although this hardly looks professional, I'm glad not to be looking at his wound.

"So this is what it's all about," I say, pretending to sink farther down into the bubbles.

Jeff and I have been married five years, but there are still moments like this. "Come here, my little water nymph," he says to me.

I'm an illegal baker, but I still take precautions. The next morning, after I preset the oven and assemble the ingredients to make Devil's Brownies—measuring out a half cup of my secret ingredient, Chocolate Malt Ovaltine—I pull my hair back into a tight bun and scrub the counters with Ajax, my hands with antibacterial soap. When the telephone rings, I let the machine answer it.

"Jesus loves you," Jesus says to me, pronouncing his name the Hispanic way. "But you're going to get your butt canned if you don't bring the man some meringues mañana."

I already feel my wrists ache from beating the whites into peaks and, irritated, turn off the oven and go for a walk. Someone has parked a pickup truck with a bumper sticker that reads *Taxpayers Revolt!* next to the curb by my house. I look across the street at the house where the bikini woman lives and watch a curtain draw shut in the front window. Too late, I smile in her house's direction.

I pass my long-faced next-door neighbor's house, whose grass is somehow both brown and in need of cutting. I pass the house of the fourth-grade teacher, who told me she watched the whole time my husband got attacked and would have come out to see how he was right then and there if she hadn't been on hold with the cable company. Instead of crossing the street and walking past the house with the billowing blue plastic covering its roof, when I near the house where the dog who bit my husband lives, I decide to stay on my side of the street. But a full house away, I hear the steady rumble of the dog's growl and turn around and head back home. In my new kitchen, I fill a bowl with egg whites and begin beating.

That night, sitting in the mossy spot where the hot tub used to be, Jeff shows me his newest splint, this one made out of the side of a cornmeal box from work, the word *corn* with just half an *n* missing, the cardboard straight across two damaged fingers.

"I think I got the angle right this time," he says. "I think we're really on the road to recovery now."

"How do we know it's really chained back there?" I say.

"Check out the moon tonight," Jeff says. "Don't you think we get a better view as homeowners?"

I look at the sky but can't find it. Inside our house, one refrigerator shelf is lined with wax paper trays of mushroom-shaped, cinnamon-dusted meringues, the secret ingredient a tablespoon of cooking sherry. I go inside and get one, bring it out for my husband and, as if both his hands were useless, feed it to him. "It wouldn't even have to be a bakery," I say. "Maybe pet grooming or a nanny service. I'm full of ideas."

"Come on," Jeff says, his mouth thick with meringue. "Give it a rest."

"Mr. Conservative," I say. "Mr. Homeowner." I push the rest of the meringue into his mouth.

Jeff chews and sinks down deeper into the place where the bubbles should be and our conversation ends.

The next day when I get home from delivering the rest of the meringues, I find yellow police tape blocking off my side street. *The dog*, I think, *has killed someone.* I park out front and find Vikkii waiting for me on my porch, blowing smoke rings at my small lime tree. "Block party," she says to me. "Everyone's counting on you for dessert."

"I don't know," I say.

"Five o'clock prompt. It used to be annual before all the bad blood," she says. "It was my idea to bring it back. Vikkii to the rescue." Then she stubs out her cigarette, hands me a flyer and walks home.

Although no one expects a dentist to give free exams just because he lives on their block, I think about *bad blood* and at five o'clock leave Jeff a note on the dining room table and walk outside with two party plates of Devil's Brownies, each wrapped in pink cellophane. Someone has tied a balloon to the police tape and set up four lawn chairs in a semicircle in the middle of the block. Without the possibility of cars driving by, the block feels eerily quiet. I put my plates of brownies on two lawn chairs and sit in a third.

I have a good view of the house where the dog who bit my husband lives, and I make out his new chain now, the silver gleaming in the sun. His owner swore he never bit anyone before, and I believed him. When he jumped the fence to bite Jeff in the hand, he did it with such purpose it was as if he had been waiting for this precise moment his entire life.

Vikkii joins me a few minutes later. She's wearing her fur-trimmed jacket and black leather pants that are a little too tight across the hips. A large green bird perches on her shoulder. She sits on the last lawn chair and helps herself to a brownie, breaks little pieces off the side and feeds them to her bird.

A door slams across the street, and my bikini-wearing neighbor descends her front steps in a long halter-top-style dress that looks as if it's made out of paisley handkerchiefs. She looks in our direction and then slowly backs up her steps, opens her door and goes back inside. "Christ," someone shouts inside the house with the billowing blue plastic roof, and then it's quiet again.

"Sometimes these things take a while to get going," Vikkii says, adjusting the shoulder on which her bird sits before helping herself to another brownie.

Later that night I finally make myself look at my husband's wound. "Be gentle," he says, as if he knows something I don't about what I'm capable of. It's scabbed over by now, two teeth mark clearly emblazoned on the back of Jeff's hand, little dotted scabs on his fingers where the dog didn't get such a good purchase. *This is my husband's hand*, I think. I massage antibacterial lotion into his fingers, then wrap his bad hand in the pink party cellophane. I'm full of ideas, but for now I keep quiet. "Screw the neighbors," Jeff says, and together we eat the rest of my block party brownies for dinner.

At eleven o'clock the party is finally underway. I watch from our bedroom window as our neighbors, accompanied by music, form a conga line down the middle of the street. "Look what you're missing out on now," Jeff says to me when I wake him, then falls back to sleep, his bad hand, still wrapped in pink cellophane, flat out on the pillow by his head. I am nowhere near tired anymore and keep on watching. On the actual block we live on, Vikkii's bird is still gripped tightly to her shoulder even as she leads the conga line, even as a car alarm goes off, and the dog that bit my husband, leashed to a streetlight now while his owner joins in, howls at it. I'm full of ideas, but, for now, I don't move.

Stampede

Looking out his sliding glass kitchen doors, Will can see that the rain has turned to sleet, and he thinks about hard pellets of ice sticking to the windshield of his daughter's car, her frozen wipers scraping over them. *Turn into a skid*, he thinks for her. *Never brake on ice.*

Colleen is driving down from Boston with her new roommate, Eric. Colleen and Eric work together at a travel agency. Something like Travel Time or Travel Trails. Colleen says that Eric, who is gay, is the perfect roommate. The ideal roommate. At night they sit up in bed and talk. "About what?" Will has asked Colleen on the phone. "About everything," Colleen told him. Will wonders what "everything" is to Colleen, if her family is part of everything. If so, then Eric knows more about him than he knows about Eric. This thought leaves Will feeling vaguely uncomfortable as he unloads the coffee cups and glasses from the dishwasher.

Will is careful with these dishes, handling them as if they were not his to drop and break. Everything he is unloading—the plain silverware; the white, rimless plates; the wide-mouthed, purposely misshapen coffee mugs—was chosen for him by his sister after his divorce. Her purchases were modern and smooth-surfaced: a sleek, teak-framed, low-to-the floor bed; beige enamel floor lamps that rise up like long, pale, hairless arms out of the carpet; even the television set, everything hidden in the screen.

Although newly and tastefully decorated, this apartment is the saddest place Will has ever lived. During the past year he has had thoughts about the emptiness of life, reasons for being—ordinary, lonely thoughts that he has dismissed as indulgent in his son, now off studying philosophy at an overpriced liberal arts college.

When the doorbell rings, Will is shaken out of his dullness. He opens the front door, and his daughter kisses him on the cheek.

"Sure is lousy weather," the boy standing next to her says, folding up his umbrella.

Will closes the door and lets his daughter and her roommate into his living room.

"Any trouble getting here?" Will asks.

"Of course not, Dad. I could drive this route in my sleep," Colleen says. "Dad, this is Eric. Eric, my dad." Colleen puts her hand on the back of her roommate's neck and pulls herself up on her toes closer to him.

For just a moment Will forgets that Eric is gay and imagines that Colleen is introducing her boyfriend to her father. And because Eric is clean-cut and friendly-enough looking, Will smiles approvingly at him before he remembers. "Nice to meet you," he says, frowning. "I understand you and Colleen work together."

"That's right. You got it, sir," Eric says. "If you don't mind, I'll just set these things down somewhere." He lifts up the suitcases he is holding a little.

"Oh, sure. Why don't you put them in the bedroom." Will points down the hall. "Just down there. You can't miss it."

While Eric is taking their suitcases into Will's bedroom, Colleen walks into the kitchen, opens the refrigerator and tells Will he should have something in the house to offer them to drink. "You could have at least bought some seltzer or something," Colleen says, closing the refrigerator door. "I guess we'll go to Giant."

"Wait, I'm sure I have something," Will says, standing next to his daughter and looking into the expanse of his refrigerator. "I know. How about some wine to celebrate your visit," Will says, reaching for a large opened bottle.

"This early?" Colleen asks. "Hey, it's okay, Dad. Don't worry about it." She rubs Will's arm gently as if, he thinks, he were a large, dumb dog. "We'll pick up some other stuff, too."

Colleen and Eric go out to the supermarket, and Will is left alone again too soon in his apartment. Feeling slightly shamed, he pours himself some wine anyway, turns on the television set and watches a pretty young woman about Colleen's age doing exercises in a blue leotard that looks too small for her. Her legs, wrapped in shiny gold tights, flash open and shut in the air. He wonders if Colleen exercises, if she's pretty to the world, her bangs cut straight and thick across her eyebrows, her cheeks always red from makeup or nature, he's not sure which.

He tries, but cannot imagine his daughter in a leotard, doesn't know if under her loose sweaters her body is shaped the way her mother's is, compact and rounded with a surprising thick crease across her belly, or in some other way—modern and hard-muscled like the exercising girl on television. Or maybe it's more like Missy's body, the woman Will's been seeing for the past three months, all long bones and thin, pronounced angles.

Colleen, Eric and Will eat spaghetti and salad in Will's kitchen, Colleen moving around refilling glasses with the red wine she and Eric bought, offering Eric and Will seconds on spaghetti while they're still eating. The phone rings while Colleen is talking about work, telling a story about a man who was looking for an airline that would let him take his dog on board with him to Cancún. Eric is helping to tell the story, imitating the man in an unnaturally high voice, bending his hand down at the wrist. Will supposes there is nothing stranger about a homosexual imitating a homosexual than there is about a Jew telling jokes about Jews or blacks calling each other names.

It's Missy on the phone. She asks Will if Colleen and her friend got there okay and says she'll call again tomorrow to see if they all might want to go to a movie or maybe to her place for dinner before they head to her mother's house. Missy, who works at the same office as Will, is thirty-four, the mid-point between Colleen's and Will's ages. She's divorced and has no children, a point in her favor. She has no caesarian section scar jutting into her abdomen, no crises with babysitters, no one in her life who is not keeping up with child support payments. Since his divorce, Will has learned something about what to look for in a woman.

"She calls too often," Will says to his daughter and Eric as he hangs up the phone.

"Who does?" Eric asks.

"This woman I've been seeing. Every night, it's her on the phone."

"Are we going to meet her?" Colleen asks. "I want to meet the mystery woman. Mom says she's very sophisticated."

"Sophisticated?" Will says. "I don't know. Your mother saw her at a cocktail party. She doesn't always dress that way. Hey, do you kids want to see something? I bet this will surprise you."

Will goes into his bedroom and comes back with a stack of brightly colored cards and envelopes. He fans them out in both hands and holds them in front of him as if he were about to demonstrate a card trick.

"These are all invitations," he says, "that I received just this month. I'm a wanted man, I can tell you that much."

"Jesus, Dad," Colleen says. "I didn't know you even knew that many people."

"I know plenty of people," Will says. "Did you kids know that divorced middle-aged men have it much easier than women in the same situation? It's a fact. Your aunt sent me an article full of statistics. Dating, remarriage, the whole kit and caboodle. Good thing for your mother she got hooked up right away. Otherwise, she would have had a tough time of it. Statistically speaking, that is."

He sits back down at the table, pushes his plate to the side, and stacks the invitations one on top of the other by size, the largest at the bottom, the smallest at the top. Then he begins restacking them, this time by date, which takes more concentration, the party in March at the bottom, the one next week at the top.

"He's right about that one, Coll. My mother hasn't had a decent date in four years," Eric says. "That's what she always says, anyway. 'Eric, sweetie, do you know how long it's been since your poor mother has had a decent date?' she says. 'It's been four years, I swear, four solid years.'" Eric imitates a sugary southern voice.

"I didn't know your mother was southern," Will says.

"Athens," Eric says. "Georgia. My dad's the one from Boston. She just followed that carpetbagger back up there like a good southern girl when they got married."

"In any case, it's not nice to make fun of your mother, son," Will hears himself saying while working on his newest pile, this one based on color—pastels at the bottom, then primaries, and, finally, black-and-white invitations on top. "I'm sure she's a fine woman."

"Jesus, Dad, Eric's only kidding," Colleen says. "Besides, who are you to tell him what he should or shouldn't say about his mother?"

"Indeed," Will says. "I'm sorry."

"Indeed?" Colleen says. "What kind of word is that?"

Will is not sure what kind of word it is, but he's a little drunk and he likes the way it sounds. "It's a good old-fashioned word," he says. "Sturdy. I'd call it a sturdy word if I had to classify it."

"Sturdy. Fine," Colleen says. She's up clearing the table, and Eric has disappeared into the kitchen with a stack of plates.

Will has begun to make a new pile, ugly women at the bottom, pretty women on top.

"I wish you wouldn't do this to me," Colleen whispers to him as she clears Will's plate.

"Do what?"

"Embarrass me in front of Eric. That's what."

"What did I do?" Will asks, looking up at his daughter.

"Forget it," Colleen says.

When Eric comes back out, Colleen asks Will where they're going to sleep.

Will looks around the apartment. There aren't a lot of options. There's his room and the living room couch that pulls out into a bed. He wonders if he should let his daughter have the bed and offer to share the couch with Eric. He doesn't know if he can do this. He's never slept in the same bed with someone gay before.

"I guess I'll take the couch, and you kids can have my room," Will says, starting a new pile, people he barely knows at the bottom, people he knew when he was still married on top.

Will lies on the sofa bed and listens to his daughter and Eric giggling in his bedroom. He cannot imagine what could be so funny, what jokes Eric could be telling to make his daughter laugh in this unfamiliar way. Perhaps he's doing voices. Maybe Eric is imitating Will's voice. He wonders how he sounds, if he is as easy to mock as the man with the little dog, as Eric's own mother. Will quietly tries out his voice, recites the alphabet, then counts to twenty, listening carefully but not discovering a characteristic distinct enough to imitate.

It's not Eric's jokes, though, that are keeping Will awake. It's his daughter's incessant giggling. For a moment the thought crosses his mind that what she needs is a good spanking, but, of course, it's much too late for that.

Will gets up and goes into the bathroom to take a sleeping pill. To alert Colleen and Eric that they are keeping him awake, he makes more noise than he has to running the water and shutting the medicine cabinet. Then he gets back into bed and tries to sleep.

At the cocktail party, he remembers, Missy wore a black, strapless, knee-length dress, and underneath it, a push-up bra, lace underpants and stockings that turned out to be held in place with thick rims of elastic that stretched around her thighs. He didn't know that his ex-wife would be there, and when he saw her walk in with the man she had left Will for, Will put his arm around Missy's shoulder and pulled her close to him, surprising them both with what Missy would later call his public display of affection.

After the party, Missy stood in his bathroom, talking about how there weren't enough appetizers and brushing her teeth, naked except for the push-up bra. His ex-wife had been very friendly to Missy. While Will shook his ex-wife's boyfriend's hand, his ex-wife shook Missy's.

Eric is already in the kitchen, reading the paper and drinking coffee, when Will finally wakes up.

"Would you like some coffee, sir?" Eric asks.

"Thank you." Will rubs his eyes and thinks that he has slept too long, rare for him. Forgetting about the sleeping pill, he wonders if they laced the spaghetti sauce with marijuana last night, something he caught his son doing once when he was still in high school.

Eric is wearing a plaid, flannel bathrobe and the backless beige kind of slippers that Will remembers his father wearing. Will's father was a serious man who drank one scotch and soda each evening while waiting for dinner to be served, and the slippers that Eric quietly shuffles across the kitchen in put Will's suspicions about the marijuana to rest. Eric hands Will his coffee already whitened with milk, although Will normally drinks his coffee black.

"Did you kids sleep okay?" Will asks.

"Oh, sure," Eric says.

"Is Colleen still sleeping?"

"No, sir, she's out running," Eric says.

"Running?" Will says.

"Sure, every morning, rain or shine," Eric says. "Puts me to shame. Do you want part of the paper?"

Although he would prefer the headlines, Will accepts the sports section. Sitting across from Eric at his kitchen table feels only slightly stranger to Will than sitting across from Missy on a weekend morning, shaking powder off the sugar donuts that she brings over the night before in her bag with her toothbrush and change of underwear.

Eric looks up from the paper once in a while and smiles, and Will sits there with his coffee, wondering if there is something neutral they could be talking about.

"So, you're from old Beantown," Will finally says.

Eric nods his head.

"That's nice," Will says. "Boston's a fine place to be from. A very collegiate city. I was happy when Colleen chose Boston."

"Right, sir," Eric says.

Will is not certain if Eric is being excessively polite or patronizing with all of his *sirs*. "I'm finding this difficult," Will says.

"Excuse me?" Eric says.

"This. Knowing what to make of all this." Will swings his arm out around the room, and Eric's eyes follow it.

"Hey, you'll be okay. You're a young guy still."

"Tell me something. If you were a woman, would you find me attractive?" Will asks.

"That's difficult for me to say, sir," Eric says.

"Right, of course," Will says, pretending to be absorbed in the hockey statistics.

That afternoon during lunch, Will remembers how he is planning to surprise his daughter before she leaves to spend the night at her mother's house. The three of them walk outside to the parking lot behind his apartment building. The sun is out now, the temperature higher, the ice melting on the blacktop.

"How do you like my new car?" Will says, pointing to a red Firebird.

"Are you kidding?" Colleen says. "You bought a Firebird?"

Eric is walking around the car, squinting into the tinted windows.

"Not really," Will says. "I had some engine trouble. The station lent me this one until mine's fixed. They just finished overhauling it. I promised to take it easy."

"Can we go for a ride?" Colleen says. "Can I drive it?"

"Sure. Why not?" Will says.

He gets in the front seat next to his daughter, and Eric sits in the back behind Colleen, leaning over her shoulder while she adjusts the seat, the rearview mirror.

"I bet your greaser boyfriends used to drive you around in cars like this," Eric says, pinching the back of Colleen's neck.

"I didn't have greaser boyfriends," Colleen says. "Did I, Dad?"

Will smiles at the windshield because he doesn't know what to say. He can't remember any of Colleen's high school boyfriends except one named Jimmy, who lived down the road from them and wore his dark hair short above the back of his neck and long over his forehead. Once Will had looked out the window after Jimmy had come by, and he had seen Colleen riding off on the handlebars of his banana-seat bicycle. Maybe Jimmy was earlier than high school.

Will directs Colleen down back roads past new developments with countrified names—Fox Pointe, Brooke Woods—and points out the pastel-colored townhouse community where Missy lives, telling Colleen not to stop now, maybe on the way back.

"It wasn't like this around here when I grew up," Colleen says to Eric. "It was mostly cornfields or something out here, I think. We never came out this way. We lived in town. There wasn't anything out here."

Will looks at his daughter, who is driving with both hands on the steering wheel. She looks smaller, sitting up straight in the broad bucket seat of the Firebird. Missy says that women today are in no hurry to settle down, but he wants his daughter settled. A rabbit hops out in front of their car, and the tires squeal as Colleen steers around it.

"What the hell was that?" Eric says from the backseat.

"A deer," Colleen says. "Didn't you see it? A big deer with antlers and everything."

"I didn't see anything," Eric says.

"You did, didn't you, Dad?" Colleen says, winking at him.

"What did you see, Mr. Barcus?" Eric says. "I bet she swerved around a ditch, that's all."

Will looks at his daughter, her hands tight on the wheel, still a good, serious driver, even today with the sun bright, the roads warming and unfrozen. He relaxes a little and stares out the side window, watching his small part of the world go by. "I saw a whole stampede of deer, all at once," he says, turning to Eric. "And I'll tell you this, I never saw them coming."

Show Me Something

Decide that the man on the balcony across the street is completely handsome. Decide this from your own balcony, which you're leaning over with some friends and a lot of strangers, throwing plastic Mardi Gras beads to people in the street and catching those tossed up to you. When you look at the man on the balcony across the street again, he aims and tosses some beads to you. The beads land in the street and are scooped up by a man dressed in drag. You know the man is a queen any day of the week because you have seen him dressed this way before, flamboyantly, wearing a beehive wig, eating wonton soup alone at the Chinese restaurant down the street.

Although you never say hello to each other at the Chinese restaurant, whistle at him now as he bends over to pick up the beads aimed at you. He waves his hanky toward your balcony. "Show us something!" someone from the street shouts up at you, and you give the asshole the finger.

Across the street, the man you decided was completely handsome is mouthing the words "Come over," and motioning with his hand. You shout back, "Come over here!" And someone else on the balcony across the street, the wrong person, a man wearing a huge duck beak on his forehead, shouts back, "Oh, baby," and gyrates his hips. Turn away in disgust. Some girl who smells like bubble gum and gin punches you in the ribs and says, "Go for it."

You get the handsome one's attention again and mouth the words, "Come over here. Now."

You go downstairs and let him and only him in through the courtyard. You notice for the first time that he is in complete costume, the upper part of his face covered with a plastic Boy Wonder mask. But when he lifts up his mask to say something to you, you see that you were right, he is good-looking, so good-looking that you don't want him to talk because he cannot be as good as he looks and so will ruin everything.

Will ruin everything that has not already been ruined, that is. You're suddenly not sure what that could be. Did you forget? Your heart is broken. Your recently ex-boyfriend, who is sorry that he's no longer in love with you, is slowly, slowly screwing someone else. You know this because you got inside his building by ringing each and every buzzer until someone finally came down to let you in, an Indian or a man dressed as an Indian, who invited you up to his party.

When your ex-boyfriend didn't answer his door, you crawled around his courtyard balcony and looked in his bedroom window. At first you thought he might be sleeping, passed out drunk, but then you saw that he was moving a little under the covers and that his elbows were supporting his head above the pillow. You watched for a while, transfixed by the image of your recently ex-boyfriend having sex, forgetting for a moment that it wasn't you he was having it with.

But then you remembered. And you banged your fist on the glass before running off. You hate him as you have never hated anyone in your entire life, and yet, of course, predictably, you still love him.

The handsome man is sitting at your kitchen table, cutting lines of coke on a mirror. You sniff up more than half before handing the dollar back to him to see what he will do, but he doesn't seem mad. You're disappointed.

"You like coke," he says, and rubs his hand up over the front of your shirt.

Idiot, you think. Still, he's got another party you can go to, so you leave everyone out on the balcony and follow him. You hold onto his Boy Wonder belt and let him lead you through the crowds. You stop at someone's apartment. You're not sure if it's his or not because you don't listen to the complicated, tedious story he tells as he unlocks the gate, leads you down a hallway and unlocks a door. You drink wine and laugh and laugh, sitting on the bed because the room is so crowded it's really more of a closet than a room. Boy Wonder thinks you're laughing at his jokes, so he tells some more. Very stupid jokes, all of them. You will not remember one of them tomorrow. You forget them even as he's telling them.

Remember, your heart is broken. Concentrate on your pain.

Sit on his lap on the edge of the bed and kiss him, pushing him down flat onto the bed covered with some girl's clothes. You think his name is Bill, but who can be sure, so don't try it out. He calls you baby, darling. It doesn't matter. He's so much the wrong person that you really could laugh again just thinking about it, his stupid body pumping under you. He takes so long to finish that you dry up. He flips you over and one, two, three, four, he's done. Your head splits in half, and you push his face away from your ear and ask where the goddamn party is anyway.

He leads you back outside into the crowds. You are wearing a hat that you took from the apartment because you had no costume and suddenly wanted one. You push the felt brim down toward your face and go to a bar and dance in front of a video screen. He wants to take up the whole crowded dance floor with his stupid moves and turns. Who does he think he is anyway? That's what you'd like to know. You shout that you're going out to buy cigarettes, but when you get outside, it's too crowded and you're pushed back in.

You find him leaning on the bar, looking around as if this whole scene is something he's observing, as if he's not even a part of it. You have never met anyone so affected. Doesn't he know your heart is breaking!

"Hey, babe, there you are," he says to you, not even shouting, but you can make out every word from across the room. That's how alone you are. You are so alone you can read Boy Wonder's lips.

You lead him out into the street, forgetting about his party because he seems to have forgotten. Let the gold-painted naked lady roller-blade past you, her dog on a leash running behind her. Don't stop to listen to the Jesus freak with the megaphone screaming about the path to salvation. Notice that this backdrop, this big, drunk party, is an extreme one for your pain.

Lead Boy Wonder back to your apartment, tossing the hat you took back-and-forth between you like a frisbee in the crowded streets. No one grabs it and runs with it. In fact, no one seems to notice you or Boy Wonder or the flying hat at all. And if they did, what would they think anyway? Probably that something was between you, the way that hat never once hit the ground.

Not for You

Betsy stops at the little church one town over on her drive down to her estranged daughter's campus. *Estranged* is the preferred word, she has learned from the online parent group, when your child is eighteen or older.

Betsy is working on not saying *missing*.

Charlotte is not missing, not like a sock or a set of keys or an umbrella. Not missing in a grocery store, her name repeated over the store's intercom system.

Charlotte is too old to be a missing face on a milk carton.

Betsy has only been to this church twice, but she is on their email list and knows today they're having a bake sale. She has made her estranged daughter's favorite cookies—peanut butter—a plate to bring to her daughter and a plate for the church. But when she walks up to the long card tables set out front, Betsy sees her mistake. Her cookies are small and misshapen, and the other cookies are as fat and round as toddlers' knees. Even her thin white paper plate is inferior to the other shiny disposable plates.

"Hello, hello," a woman with a face as doughy and circular as the good cookies says. "Did you want to donate those?"

"No," Betsy says. "I don't think so."

"Oh," the woman says, her face deflating. "Well," she says. "We'd love to sell them if you change your mind. All proceeds go to the Sunday school."

Betsy scans the long card tables lined with flawless baked good—lemon bars topped with candied lemons, sugar cookies with M&M faces, gingerbread men iced in luminescent sugared swim trunks and flip-flops.

"And to support our little church camp," the woman adds.

What could stop anyone from poisoning their cookies? Betsy wonders. At Charlotte's old elementary school, a note went home on bright pink paper with **Nothing Homemade!** shouted across the top of the page, a celebration instead admonishment. Maybe this was earlier than elementary school. Maybe it was a note from that preschool by the pond where Charlotte had begged to feed the ducks on their way home even though this wasn't allowed either.

Don't Feed the Ducks! shouted another paper. Betsy read the note to her daughter when they got home. She heard the excessive cheeriness in her own voice, as if she were reading a birthday party invitation instead of a lecture.

"It was better the way it used to be before the stupid preschool," Charlotte said with the kind of sigh more familiar in a defeated adult than a three-year-old child. And Betsy knew her daughter was right. It was better when it was just the two of them, feeding the ducks, when they could rip apart soft white chunks of cheap bread for the ducks to fight over without worrying about the ecosystem, without worrying about the spongy bread expanding and bloating the ducks' delicate bellies.

Despite Charlotte walking away, Betsy continued reading the entire preschool note aloud. She read about still visiting with the ducks from the shore, watching them paddle behind each other across the pond, the way water rolled off their oily backs. She read the note's operatic crescendo of an ending about the circle of life and how humans were only a small piece of everything, a part of nature ourselves.

"We used to feed them!" her daughter shouted from her room before slamming the door. "Why can't you just bring bread when you pick me up?"

Betsy purchases a brownie so evenly shellacked with frosting it looks plastic. "That will be fifty cents," the woman behind the table says, her deflated face opening up again as she smiles and reaches out her palm for the coins Betsy has dug out of the bottom of her purse.

The woman is counting out the nickels and dimes. "Oops, someone has given me too much money," she says.

Betsy looks around, but she's still the only one there. "You can keep the change," Betsy says. "For the children." The brownie is wrapped so tightly in plastic wrap Betsy thinks about suffocation. She feels her own throat constrict. It occurs to her that something awful has happened to her daughter, that she should have called the police months ago. *What is wrong with her?*

"Are you sure I can't take those?" the woman says, nodding at Betsy's plate of cookies.

"They're not for you," Betsy says, the plastic wrap on her sagging plate of cookies loose and already opening on one side.

"I meant for our sale. For our little Sunday school. Do you have children?"

Betsy backs away. She walks backwards down two steps and out to her car, the brownie balanced on top of her own plate of cookies, centered on top like a small brick.

In the car, Betsy calls her husband's cell phone. Greg's a mortgage broker, and he used to work in an office, but now he mostly works at home. By commuting less, he says he's doing his part to limit his carbon footprint, but Betsy knows this isn't the real reason. She has seen him online updating the listserv and staring out at their empty street, watching for crime.

"What," Greg says, a statement instead of a question.

"Why didn't we call the police?" she says.

"We're registered," he says. "We're an official Neighborhood Watch."

"I mean about her." But she remembers now that they don't talk about Charlotte's absence. That's all they talked about for the first month when her daughter left in the middle of spring break, disappeared without saying goodbye, angry at Betsy who insisted she get out of bed, take a shower, move on from that boy at college.

Enough, give her space, her husband had said. *Give me space.*

"We did call the police," Greg says now. "Jesus, how don't you remember? 'No foul play,' they said. 'No evidence. She's over eighteen.'"

Betsy sinks back into the seat of her car. How could she not have remembered the police in her living room not writing down anything, instead standing there over them as she and Greg sat on the couch, talking to them as if they were children themselves. Telling them this happens, grown children sometimes need space, give it some time.

Betsy unwraps the brownie.

"What's wrong with you?" her husband says.

Betsy understands that this isn't a question Greg expects her to answer, that, in fact, it isn't a question at all. Her husband doesn't ask her questions anymore. He barely talks to her at all unless he's talking about neighborhood crime. *When did this happen?* she wonders. The inside of the plastic wrap is slick and slides right off. Betsy licks the plastic, which tastes like cheap, fragrant oil.

"I'm hanging up," Greg says, but instead he keeps talking. "Did you know that thieves can break into cars wirelessly now? People leave their fobs by the front door, and they may as well be leaving their cars unlocked."

Betsy puts the phone down on the seat next to her, where her two plates of cookies—the one she no longer plans to drop off at the bake sale and the one she still plans to take to her daughter—sit side by side again, and bites into the brownie. Although they live in a neighborhood where children kick soccer balls in their front yards and run out to wave to the garbagemen on trash days, her husband has become obsessed with neighborhood crime. He is considering adding bars to their first-floor windows.

*What's wrong with **you**?* she doesn't say to him.

She hears him talk on and on, and then finally stop.

The brownie is dry and sweet in a chemical-tasting way, as if the baker substituted something low calorie in place of sugar.

Or maybe the baker has substituted drugstore perfume. Betsy looks at her phone and sees she has five unanswered texts from her mother, who is planning an anniversary party for Betsy and her husband, a marriage that Betsy now understands is over. Although he's home more than he's gone, like Charlotte, Greg has already left her.

Betsy's mother has had many questions about flowers and balloons and appetizers, pass-through or station. Betsy doesn't open the new texts. Instead she sits in her car eating the brownie and watches from her car window as a family walks up to the bake sale, a little girl between two adults swinging her off the ground every third step they take, the girl's hands gripped tight, one each, in theirs. *Stop*, Betsy thinks, although she doesn't know exactly what she wants this little family to stop doing. "Stop," she says aloud.

Betsy's overnight bag is already in the trunk, but she drives back toward her own neighborhood again. To avoid seeing her husband, who is certainly hunched over his computer, updating the Neighborhood Watch list or pricing out security bars, Betsy parks a block away from their street.

She walks with her plate of peanut butter cookies up to the front door of the rental house on her block with the new renters. A few days earlier she had scared the little girl who lives there, telling her she was playing with Charlotte's discarded baby dolls left over from a yard sale, that they didn't belong to her. She remembers the little girl's mother opening the front door and glaring at her.

What's wrong with you? her husband said when she tried to tell him what had happened.

Betsy thinks now she will make it right, that she will show the neighbors that nothing is wrong with her. She will knock at the door and say hello, welcome to the neighborhood, and I'm sorry if I scared your little girl the other day.

The little girl has left a doll on the front lawn. Betsy recognizes its blank eyes and matted hair, its plastic limbs extending from its soft, stuffed body. One of Charlotte's discarded dolls. She will hand the doll to the mother with the cookies. *Hello*, she will say. *Just wanted to say welcome to the neighborhood. I made you some cookies.*

But a dog barks from inside, and Betsy drops the cookies and runs.

Betsy is in her car now and driving south, her heart pounding, the neighbor's doll, once her daughter's doll, in the seat next to her. They are heading to her daughter's college. The college administration told her nothing. "I'm sorry," a man said on the phone, when Betsy said she just wanted to know if her daughter had dropped out of her classes or not. "There are privacy laws. We're not allowed to give you that kind of information. FERPA."

"Have you seen my daughter?" Betsy asked. "Can you just tell me that? She has long brown hair, and she walks with her head down when she's sad. Maybe her hair is shorter now," Betsy said, remembering a mother in the online support group for *estranged* children who didn't recognize her own daughter when she ran into her in line at a 7/11, the daughter's earlobes stretched round and thin with plugs.

That's what they're called, that mother had typed in the chat. *I looked them up. I didn't recognize her in line, and then when I finally did, she was out the door. She bought cigarettes*, the mother continued. *She doesn't smoke. Do you know what cigarettes cost now? Where did she get the money?*

"I'm sorry," the man on the phone said.

Betsy thought he sounded very young, as if maybe he were a student himself, or had just graduated. "Is there anyone else there who can help me?" Betsy asked.

"I'm sorry," he repeated. "No one is allowed to give out student information. None of us."

"Maybe she did something to her ears," Betsy said. "Or she has tattoos now." Another missing child in the group has tattoos called sleeves that stretch up their arms.

"I'm sure you'll hear from her soon."

"How can you be sure?" Betsy said. "Do you know something?"

"I guess that's the wrong word," the man said. "I should have said I *hope* you hear from her soon. I'm not supposed to advise you, but you know our campus is open. You can just show up if you want, if you feel that worried."

And, now, two months later, three months after her daughter has been estranged, disappeared from her bedroom over spring break when all Betsy did was encourage her to come out of her room, to shake off a boy from college who had hurt her, Betsy is finally showing up. She would have showed up sooner, but Greg said to give their daughter space.

"You're only going to end up making things worse," he said. "Let her breathe. You suffocate everyone. Why do you have to suffocate everyone?"

So Betsy tried to let their daughter breathe. At first she left texts and voicemails and emails and Facebook messages. *Is everything okay?* she asked. *I just want to know you're okay.*

To let her daughter breathe, Betsy replaced these messages by telegraphing through thought-waves. *Good night*, she whispered each night, opening her daughter's bedroom door and speaking into the dark. For two months she has felt her own breath catch ragged in her throat while she has let her daughter breathe. She walks into her daughter's empty room each morning. She pulls open the curtains. *Good morning. I hope you slept well.*

The college is only a three-hour drive away. Betsy cannot believe she hasn't done this sooner. This is what's wrong with the parents in the support group. They have been waiting when they should have been looking. They don't even recognize their own children. No wonder their children have left them. She will delete this group of whiners as soon as she gets home. They have been no help. She sees that now.

Betsy is charged up with purpose. She feels a glancing moment of nausea, the slick brownie she ate earlier moving up through her body, and thinks about pulling over and throwing up, but she swallows hard, opens her window and keeps driving, warm air rushing in on her face.

Betsy parks easily and walks toward her daughter's dorm, carrying peanut butter cookies for her daughter. The plate is warm from the car, as if the cookies have just come out of the oven. The sun is out, but no one is sunbathing or playing frisbee on the lawn. Betsy thinks everyone must be in classes. A single student walks by. For a second, Betsy thinks the student is talking to her, but then she sees the girl's ears are stuffed with wireless headphones.

When Betsy gets to her daughter's dorm building, she pulls on the door, but the building is locked, and there is no one sitting at the front desk to buzz her in. Betsy peers in and around the corner into the empty study lounge, chairs flipped over on top of tables, the carpet vacuumed in neat, even lines.

Betsy realizes her mistake. The semester is over. She has missed the end by days or weeks. How could she not know? She waited too long, and now she doesn't know where to look for her daughter who she did not come to pick up the way she should have when the semester ended, loading the car with unwashed bedding and taped-up boxes, a microwave greasy from popcorn.

When her phone rings, Betsy answers without looking for a name, thinking it must be Charlotte, finally. After all, she's at her daughter's school now. Even if she's not here, her daughter must know this. But her own mother is on the other end.

"So you exist," her mother says. "I was beginning to wonder."

"I can't talk now. I'm right in the middle of something."

"I just have a few questions about the party," her mother says. "How do you feel about a roving violinist? White wine versus Prosecco?"

"I'll call you back," Betsy says. "My battery is dying." She is sitting on the ground now, and maybe she has hung up the phone and maybe she hasn't. A rat crosses the empty lawn in front of where Betsy sits and stops and stares at her. "Oh, you're a possum," Betsy says. "Not any prettier."

The animal stares at Betsy so long, she wonders if it's trying to communicate with her. One of the missing adult children from the parent support group has gone off in search of her spirit animal, a coyote. The girl has been following the coyote through the San Bernardino Mountains. She left with a small backpack, the kind you carry instead of a purse. *She was wearing sandals,* the online mother wrote. *Flip-flops, really. I don't know if she even brought a sweater.*

"Go away," Betsy says to the possum. "Aren't you supposed to be nocturnal? I don't want you. You are not my spirit animal." She throws a peanut butter cookie as far as she can, hoping the possum will head away from her to eat it, but instead the possum runs toward her, as if for protection, as the cookie flies over its head.

Betsy drops the rest of the cookies and runs through the empty campus, back toward the safety of her car. The possum isn't chasing her, but she feels its form in the air behind her. *Run,* it's saying. *Let's go, let's go, let's go.*

Betsy gets in her car and locks the doors. She is breathing heavily. On the seat facedown next to her is the doll. She turns it over and sees her mistake. It was never Charlotte's doll. Its flat blue eyes are painted on, and its face is ruddy. She would never buy her daughter a doll like this.

She rolls down the windows and starts to throw the doll out in the parking lot before taking off. Maybe this is littering. Instead, she tosses it in the backseat. She opens up "Maps" on her phone but doesn't know what to enter.

Girl, she types. And Girl Scouts pops up.

Daughter. Daughter's Deli.

Help gives her a phone number instead of a place. Helpline. She pushes the button. "Hello," she says, before anyone answers. "Thank you," she says when someone does. She hangs up and ignores the phone call she gets back.

We're here if you still need us, someone from Helpline texts.

Betsy imagines a volunteer, a woman who looks like her but with a daughter who is not estranged. Maybe her daughter is sitting next to her, volunteering, too. Together, when their shift is over, they will go home and, over chamomile tea or a well-deserved glass of wine, talk about all the pathetic people they helped.

The woman is a better person than Betsy, who has volunteered very little in her life. She didn't even leave her cookies at the bake sale, instead, scattering them across a neighbor's lawn. When her daughter was in elementary school, she was scheduled to help out once a week in Charlotte's classroom, but this was, in truth, more spying than volunteering.

Betsy edges her car out of the nearly empty parking lot as if the lot is full of cars she has to be careful not to hit. She asks her phone for directions to the freeway and points her car where she is told. She listens to the voice confidentially mispronounce the names of streets.

It's me again, she types back to Helpline at a red light.

Hello? Betsy types. *Hello. Is anyone there?*

It's dark now, and Betsy is following Google Maps to the freeway heading south. She'll get away from this place and make a plan. She'll become a better person, someone who answers a Helpline or ladles out food for the homeless every Friday night at a church. Maybe she'll join the church near her with the bake sale. Can you join a church? Or do you just go? She doesn't know. There is so much Betsy doesn't know. She stops at another light.

Hello? she types.

What happened to being there?

If she worked for Helpline, Betsy would text back. She would call back. She would not disappear because her shift was over.

Charlotte would see how deserving she is of love.

The motel where Betsy checks in has chocolate chip cookies on a plate under a glass cover on the counter. The cover is tall and bell-shaped, and maybe the cookies look even smaller because they are under it. A reverse magnifying glass. It's a cake cover really. That's what it is. The cookies are nothing like the show-offy ones at the church bake sale with their hand-etched pastel icing. Probably they are just slice-and-bake. Probably they taste like the inside of a refrigerator.

Still, Betsy wants one. Except for a brownie from the church bake sale, she hasn't eaten all day, and now it's night. She grabs hold of the round glass ball on top of the glass cover. She lifts it up too quickly, and she realizes her mistake, that the cover is plastic. It reminds her of lifting up a plastic beer mug years ago and slinging the beer over her shoulder in surprise.

Betsy is surprised by so many things, each an example of how wrong she has been, her perceptions not to be trusted. Her own nineteen-year-old daughter has not spoken to her in months, choosing to sneak out of her own house in lieu of having lunch with her. Betsy grabs a cookie while she is waiting for the woman behind the desk to run her credit card. She smells its distinct absence of flavor before taking a bite.

Maybe Betsy has felt lonelier in her life, but she cannot remember when.

Maybe when her daughter first disappeared.

Maybe when her husband first turned away from her.

She's not sure which one happened first. Maybe they happened at the same time, but probably not. Betsy's past is as hazy and caramel-scented as a drugstore candle.

"You'll see a hold for a hundred dollars on your card," the young woman checking her in says. Crystal. Crystal wears her name on a chain around her neck. She looked up from her phone when Betsy entered the small lobby, and Betsy read her name in gold-hued cursive. Then Crystal looked down, scrolled, and frowned, and typed something into her phone and sent it off with a familiar swoosh.

She is younger than Betsy but older than Betsy's missing daughter. Maybe she's in her late twenties. Maybe she's younger than that. She's not fat, but she's overweight enough that her face is plumped smooth and creaseless. Betsy wonders if Crystal has children yet, if she has a daughter with milky breath who grabs her hand when they cross the street.

"For incidentals. It'll fall off after you check out."

"What kind of incidentals do you have here?" Betsy asks. She noticed a small pool across from the office, but she hadn't noticed a restaurant.

"You don't have to be like that," Crystal says.

"I didn't mean anything," Betsy says, feeling herself fidgeting from her unintentional rudeness. "I just wondered. Are these cookies free? May I have another?"

Crystal sighs and hands Betsy back her credit card. "One or two keys?" she says.

Betsy holds up her index finger. She remembers it's called a pointer. She doesn't trust herself to talk. Who knows what she'll say next?

Betsy is relieved when Crystal hands her an actual key instead of some programmed card that may or may not work.

"Replacement is twenty dollars if you lose it," she says.

"Ah, an incidental," Betsy says and smiles, but she sees that Crystal has misinterpreted her smile and looks even more annoyed with her.

"If that's all," Crystal says, but it's not a question. She's picked up her phone and is already turning her back and heading into her office. Betsy sees a desk in there piled with papers, a small TV, or maybe it's a computer screen, propped up on top of some kind of manuals.

"No, that's perfect," Betsy says, but Crystal is already seated and doesn't bother turning around.

Betsy drives her car down through the parking lot until she comes to her numbered room. There are just a few other cars in the lot, and she parks right outside her door. Her husband would never stay here now on the first floor of a motel where anyone could barge right into your door without even entering a hallway first. When they were first married, he wouldn't have cared. He would have slept with this sliding window wide open, and Betsy would have had to pull the blinds shut when he got out of the shower and walked through the bedroom naked.

But now there are thefts in their neighborhood. He installed a lock on their mailbox, a sign in their front yard, alarms on their windows, a camera in their doorbell. He heads up the neighborhood watch. He is the captain. Sometimes Betsy can hear him typing on his keyboard late at night. When she's half asleep, it sounds like rain, and she thinks about their lawn and how it needs watering. The automatic sprinklers are no longer automatic. Probably she should talk to the gardeners about fixing them, an item from a long list she doesn't accomplish.

When Betsy checks the neighborhood listserv, she sees what her husband has posted at two in the morning. *Neighbors: Do not allow your children to leave their bicycles on your front porches. Locked or unlocked, you are inviting thieves. Did you remember to order your Neighborhood Watch window sticker? Did you order your lawn sign? There's still time to get your order in.*

Betsy picked the motel because she was tired and running low on gas and had seen the sign from the interstate, MOTEL. Lit up in yellow off the exit ramp. Maybe she should have at least asked for the second floor. But she won't go back and talk to Crystal. Even though Betsy does, in fact, have questions. She wants to know if there's coffee in the lobby in the morning. She wants to know what time she has to check out. She wants to know if there's someplace nearby to get dinner. She wants to know who else is behind these doors and if she will hear them through her walls. If they'll blast their televisions or scream into their cell phones or pound into each other's bodies.

She hopes there will be noise.

But so far she hears none. She deadbolts her door, but the latch feels flimsy, the screws loose in their plate in the wall, so she pushes a wheeled desk chair up against her door, understanding the futility of this gesture. Then she texts her husband.

I haven't found Charlotte yet. Spending the night at a motel.

She stares at her phone, waiting for a response, for questions that don't come about the motel, about when she'll be home, and then she shuts it off.

Her laptop searches for a signal, and Betsy finds it by the bathroom. She sits on the floor with her back against the bathroom door and types in her daughter's name—a stupid plan, no plan at all really. Their daughter is missing. Probably she had just gone back to college, but when Betsy went to look for her, she found out college had ended for the semester. What kind of mother was she not to know this?

There is a woman who lives not far from here with her daughter's name who gives motivational speeches. They appear to be generic. **Seize the day. Find time to breathe. Invite change into your life.** Betsy had found her before when she was searching for her daughter online. She's seen this Charlotte's picture under Google Images.

Betsy stumbles into her again now. This Charlotte wears blouses with thick silk neck ties built into them that she loops into fat bows. Her hair is flat and blond and bobbed, her face is as open as a cupcake. She looks nothing like Betsy's Charlotte with her slouch and loose tee shirts. But she's the only Charlotte Betsy has. Her own daughter is as elusive to Betsy online as she is in life.

Instead, there is only this woman, out there in the world with her daughter's first and last name. Betsy navigates her way to the young woman's website, finds the contact link and sends her a message. *Hello,* she writes. *How did you get into the motivational speaking business? Would you be open to an interview?*

Betsy closes her computer, feeling more tired now than hungry. She lies down on the bed, which is covered in a thin bedspread with a peacock embroidered on it. It's a surprisingly delicate bedspread, a thin quilt really, in this otherwise unremarkable room. Betsy kicks off her shoes, unhooks her bra, and falls asleep quickly for the first time in weeks, as if nothing of substance is weighing on her.

In the morning, she's not disoriented by the strange room or by the fact that she's slept with her clothes on. Instead, she feels an unfamiliar energy. She opens her suitcase and undresses, then pulls on her bathing suit. She packed it, imagining a beachy reunion with her daughter, a mother/daughter picnic of greasy fries and milkshakes under a rented umbrella. Or maybe blended juices. Her daughter used to like those. They had some kind of rhyming berry names. Or maybe they were alliterative. Fruity Tutty. Bananarama.

Betsy feels a sinking doom begin to descend and grabs a towel from her bathroom and takes off before the feeling claims her. She walks barefoot through the parking lot toward the front of the building, where she saw a small rectangular pool surrounded by a metal fence. The cement area around the pool is devoid of furniture.

Betsy bends down and tests the water with her fingertips. The water's cold, but she has no idea what temperature. The air is cold, too, the marine layer still thick. Betsy doesn't know how close to the ocean the motel is, but the fog makes it feel closer than she thought it was. Betsy isn't sure which is colder, the air or the water, but she doesn't care. She's never cared, always quick to shed her jacket. Cold has always had the power to wake her. She dives into the motel pool, surfacing nearly on the other end, sinks back under and kicks off from the side.

Betsy had nearly forgotten how much she used to like swimming before her daughter was born. After Charlotte, every moment at a beach required a militaristic vigilance—crashing waves and bigger children grabbing buckets, and always the lookout for men standing on the shore without their own children to watch out for. Before all that, Betsy would wade out into the bay and swim laps, passing the orange buoys that denoted the swimming area, touching one with her curled palm as if petting a stray cat.

When Betsy finishes swimming, she pulls herself out of the deep end of the pool and sees a man dressed in a white oxford shirt and pastel shorts sitting on a chair facing her. He is smiling down at her. The chair is straight backed and looks as if it belongs to a matching dining room set. The man sits up so erect in the chair, he almost appears to be mocking his own posture.

"You're not a bad swimmer," he says in an accented voice.

"Thank you," Betsy says, more a question that a statement.

"Usually it's empty, or there's a bunch of kids flailing about. Once there was an obese man floating on his back. From the office, I thought it was a pregnant woman."

Betsy thinks about the pregnant woman who opened up someone's gate and floated on her own raft in a backyard pool in her neighborhood, how Betsy's husband posted this on the listserv of stolen items with the rusted scooters and kicked-off roller skates, but she doesn't share this story.

"Excuse me," she says. But the man doesn't back his chair up, and Betsy is forced to either jump back in the pool or walk by him.

"That wasn't a pretty picture," he says in his accent. British maybe. "His white belly poking out like that. Believe you me."

The marine layer cleared while Betsy was swimming, and the sun's early brightness has momentarily bleached Betsy's towel into the cement, but she finally spots it and walks a few feet to grab it. Feeling the man's eyes on her, she quickly wraps it around her waist, although it's so small it barely reaches.

"Enjoy your morning," he shouts as she walks away.

Betsy walks quickly to her room, locks her door behind her, and hooks the flimsy deadbolt. She wheels over the desk chair, sits down on it, leans back against the door, and stares at the wet footprints across the carpet with alarm before realizing they're her own.

They are splotchy, nothing like the fragile surface prints she would have made with her daughter in the sand.

Betsy catches her breath ragged from swimming or fear, she isn't sure which, and spots her cell phone where she left it plugged in on the night table. There are two messages, both from her mother, who is planning an anniversary party for Betsy's marriage, which is now, it is clear to Betsy, over.

How do you feel about lemongrass chicken?

Are you free to meet with the florist on Thursday?

Betsy ignores the text messages and finds her computer by the bathroom and checks her email. She has heard back from the woman with her daughter's name, the motivational speaker. *I love to give interviews!* the woman has written. *What outlet are you with?*

Don't end a sentence with a preposition, Betsy wants to write. But instead she types, *I'm independent.* And she feels for the first time in a long time that maybe she is. Independent. No one is checking on her whereabouts, although she supposes her mother will eventually, probably before her husband does.

Betsy believes she feels the motivational speaker who shares her daughter's name pausing. Betsy thinks about adding that she wrote for her student newspaper. But this was over two decades ago.

Maybe the motivational speaker is sitting with her computer on her lap in her backyard full of hummingbirds and night-blooming jasmine, writing an important new speech about the meditative beauty to be found in nature. Or she's off for a brisk jog through her neighborhood or taking her perpetually smiling poodle-mix dog on a hike in the mountains. Betsy has studied her website and knows more about her than any of her actual neighbors despite her husband's neighborhood watch. *Looking forward to hearing from you*, Betsy writes, and then pushes send.

The chlorine has left a film on Betsy's skin, but she decides to skip a shower and get dressed. In truth, she doesn't really decide anything. She is thinking of the man by the pool and how the lock on her door isn't strong enough to keep out someone intent on pushing that door open.

When she checks out, Betsy is surprised to find this man behind the counter. "Where's Crystal?" she asks. Betsy feels her heart race. Has he done something with Crystal?

"I don't suppose I know," he says. "Doing whatever she does when she's not sitting on her large rump, scaring away the customers."

Betsy wants to tell him that he's much scarier than Crystal, but she realizes that she's wrong. He's not scary at all. She gets so much wrong. "I don't know. She didn't exactly scare me. But I'm a terrible judge of character."

"Don't sell yourself short," he says. "You seem a perfectly good judge of character to me. My son, now he's not much of a judge of character. Crystal's my daughter-in-law. He got his own place and job, and I'm stuck with her now, it seems. Off to see your daughter maybe?"

"Excuse me?" Betsy says.

"For the long weekend?"

Betsy had no idea it was a long weekend until this moment. "Why would you say that?"

"You just seem the type."

"What type is that?" Betsy asks, feeling not at all sure she wants to hear his answer.

"I guess the mother-of-a-daughter type," he says. "Tea time and dress shopping and all that. My ex-wife always wanted a daughter, but all we got was a son. And now I suppose she would have had Crystal if she'd stuck around."

"I don't have children," Betsy says.

"Sorry, I shouldn't make assumptions. I know what they say about 'assume.' Makes an ass, et cetera, et cetera. Well, enjoy your long weekend wherever you're going."

"No cookies this morning?" Betsy says, staring at the empty plate covered with the glass bell jar.

"Afternoons only," he says, handing her a sheet of paper with her checkout information. "Tea time," he adds and winks.

"Why do you do that?" Betsy asks.

"Do what?"

"Wink. You shouldn't wink at customers. And you shouldn't stare at them when they're swimming. You make people uncomfortable. Is that okay in England or wherever you're from?"

Betsy watches his face deflate.

"Australia," he says. "I'm from Australia."

She has never been mean before, but Betsy feels mean now. And she feels the power in it. Why hadn't she tried this before? "Well, I don't know what's normal in Australia, but it's rude here to stare at people and to wink at them and to make assumptions. No wonder you have hardly any customers here. Also, you should have coffee. And cookies in the morning, too. Or muffins. Those little ones at least."

He gives Betsy a salute, or maybe he's just reaching up to scratch his forehead.

Betsy feels her knees begin to buckle. She thinks about the word *buckle*. It's something sing-songy on an old shoe, one, two, but now it's happening to her knees.

When Betsy opens her eyes, Crystal is standing over her. Her necklace is dangling in front of Betsy's face, and she can smell the sweet saltiness of Crystal's breath.

"When is the last time she's eaten?" Crystal is asking, and the words are not echoing exactly, but they're indistinct, as if there's a visible shadow surrounding them.

"How would I know?" the father-in-law says.

Betsy hears herself asking her daughter these same words when she was small. *When is the last time you ate?* She remembers trying to tempt her with a bribe. *Eat something. And then you can watch TV. And then you can go back outside to play.*

Not all children are food driven, the pediatrician said at her daughter's third-year physical. They watched Charlotte choose a smiley-face sticker over a fruit-infused lollipop after her checkup. *She'll eat when she gets hungry.*

And she did. When she got hungry enough she ate the cheese sticks or the apples or the buttered pasta Betsy put in front of her, all with equally joyless resolution.

"Last night," she says. "I had those cookies."

"Well, that's hardly eating," Crystal says.

"I'm sorry," Betsy says.

"You know I was enrolled in some pre-nursing classes before someone up and left and left me broke, and it's obvious what you have is low blood sugar."

Betsy is sitting up, and the man with the accent is handing her a bottle of water. "I'm so much trouble," Betsy says, nice again. She stares at a dark spot on the wall that may or may not be dried blood, trying to find her balance. Being mean has led to this. Sitting on this lobby floor.

Crystal is silent, but Crystal's father-in-law is saying, "No trouble, no trouble at all. We're locking up and getting you something to eat. That's what we're doing. You're the last one checking out today."

And then Betsy is in the backseat of a car with the seat next to her full of old magazines—*McCall's* and *Family Circle* and *Fly Fisherman*—and Crystal is driving and Crystal's father-in-law is in the seat next to Crystal, his window open wide and his elbow leaning against the frame, his fingers tapping on the roof of the car. His knees are raised up. He not only has good posture, he is oddly tall, what her mother would call all limbs. Why has Betsy not noticed this until now? She feels like their child back here, even though she can see now that Crystal can't be much older than her own daughter, and she has no idea how old this man is. She doesn't even know his name.

The restaurant they take her to is square-shaped with square tables, and they sit at a table overlooking the parking lot that surrounds the restaurant. Betsy looks out at the cars and empty spaces and realizes she has no idea what the car they drove in here looks like. "The usual, Ben?" the waitress says, and Betsy learns his name this way. "What are you girls having?" she asks.

Betsy is confused for a moment at being called a girl, but Crystal speaks right up and orders pancakes with strawberries and light whipped cream. When it's Betsy's turn, she is lost in the tall laminated menu with its dense type. "She should get something with protein," Crystal says.

"The lady will have a hamburger. And fries," Ben says.

Lady. Girl. Relieved to be free of decisions, Betsy hands the waitress her menu.

"And a black-and-white," Ben says, winking at the waitress.

"A what?" Betsy says.

"It's a milkshake. You'll like it."

Crystal is busy on her phone, typing and posing with her cheeks pulled in and taking pictures. Selfies. Betsy never saw Charlotte do this although she has, of course, seen other girls posing into their phones. Most of the girls aren't any prettier than Charlotte, but they preen—yes, that's the word Betsy is looking for—like they're models. Like this pudgy Crystal is doing right now. Was it just last night that Betsy was afraid of her?

Their food arrives quickly, and Betsy watches Ben poke open his egg yolks with his fork and Crystal circle syrup over her strawberry-topped pancakes. Betsy takes a sip of an enormous milkshake, the fluted glass sweating in her palm, and works on swallowing. Shouldn't they have given her a straw? Her hamburger may as well be made of plaster, but she bites into it and chews and smiles at Ben, who's done the ordering.

"What did I tell you," he says.

"Delicious," Betsy lies. "Everything."

Now Crystal is photographing her pancakes. Then she is eating with gusto, that's the word Betsy is looking for. She envies Crystal her enthusiasm for food. "My daughter never really enjoyed food," Betsy says.

"I thought you didn't have children," Ben says.

"Why would you think that?" Betsy says.

"That's what you told me," Ben says.

She feels both Ben and Crystal staring at her, Crystal's pancake-covered fork held in mid-air above her necklace. And then she remembers. He had asked her about the long weekend. "Well," Betsy says.

"So, do you have a daughter or don't you?" Crystal asks. She is chewing now but has generally turned her interest from her phone to Betsy. "I don't get it."

Betsy thinks about the parents in the chat room for abandoned parents, the words they advise using to explain. "We're estranged. For now."

"Oh," Crystal says. "Like me and my husband. Why didn't you just say so?"

"She just did," Ben says.

"I wanted kids right away but Tommy didn't. It's one of the reasons he moved out. He's got to get his head on straight before he comes back."

"One of many reasons," Ben says.

Betsy hears her phone ringing in her purse. She retrieves it from the bottom and reads the words *Maybe Charlotte Warner* across the screen. She feels as if she might pass out again. She has never been a fainter, but maybe now she is. Maybe A Fainter. She hasn't spoken to her daughter in three months. "Hello," she says, getting up from the table and searching for the front door. "Are you there? Charlotte?"

"Is this Betsy Warner?" a woman's voice says.

This is your mother, Betsy wants to say. But she barely recognizes her own daughter's voice. "Yes, of course," Betsy says. "Who else would it be?" Instantly, Betsy regrets her words, her tone, answering the call at all. She should have let it go to voicemail and called back after she had a chance to gather herself. She is standing in a parking lot, the sun beating down on her, two strangers waiting inside a restaurant for her to come back and finish her lunch.

"I'm sorry," Betsy says. "I'm just surprised you called me."

"Well, you gave me your number."

And then Betsy understands she doesn't recognize this voice because it's not her daughter's voice at all. It's the Charlotte Warner of sunshine and motivation and squeezing the pulp out of each moment. "Oh," Betsy says. "It's you. Charlotte Warner."

"The very same!" the voice says, regaining its perkiness.

Betsy imagines this Charlotte Warner outside in her butterfly-and-hummingbird garden, surrounded by night-blooming jasmine and phlox and bluestar. Betsy has never planted a successful garden. When Charlotte was younger, the preschool sent home wildflower seeds and they littered them across their patchy front lawn and watched the neighborhood song sparrows swoop down to eat them that same day.

"Did you want to set up an interview time?"

"Right," Betsy says. Betsy looks back at the restaurant, sees her own mottled reflection in the glass. She wonders if they've cleared away her hamburger, her French fries, her black-and-white. Suddenly, she can imagine eating all of it and ordering more. Maybe what she's been feeling all along is hunger, that deep yearning and sinking nothing more than a need for calories. "I have a lot of questions," Betsy says. "For my article."

"We can meet in my garden if you'd like," the woman who has her daughter's name says. "Some people like to photograph me there."

"Amid the phlox and bluestar," Betsy says.

"Excuse me?" the wrong Charlotte says. Betsy hears the motivational speaker's voice tighten and crisp the same way her daughter's did when Betsy said too much. When she interfered and drove her own daughter away.

"I just saw the pictures. On your website. How's tomorrow?"

"Well, it's a holiday weekend, but I suppose I can make myself available."

Betsy memorizes the address and hangs up, then sees her husband has sent her a new text: *When you left yesterday you didn't lock the deadbolt. You've got to do better.*

I fainted but I'm fine now, Betsy writes back, stuffs the phone in her purse and walks back inside the restaurant.

Crystal sighs when she sees Betsy, and Ben is already standing, a white plastic bag gripped in one hand.

"Well, I hope that was important," Crystal says. She's gripping her own plastic bag as she stands up.

"We got you packed up," Ben says. "Got to get back to the office." He hands her the bag he's holding, and Betsy sees her milkshake on the table, melted down now—it looks like streaky brown ink. How did she drink this? How could she have thought she wanted the food in this bag?

"How much do I owe you?" Betsy says.

"Don't worry about it." Ben starts to wink at her, and then she sees him stop mid-wink, pretend to wipe something off his eyebrow.

Betsy gets in the car and sets her bag filled with leftovers on top of the pile of old magazines in the seat next to her. The hamburger smell is overwhelming in the sealed car, but the back windows are locked. "I'm also estranged from my husband," she says. She thinks about adding "for now" but decides against it.

"Well, look at you," Crystal says. "And I thought my life sucked." Crystal pulls the car over in front of a low-rise coral-colored apartment building. "Be right back," she says.

"He's a shithead, my son," Ben says. "Already had other girls over there. I've had to listen to her go on all about it. But she hasn't given up. Ordered him his own meal, and I end up paying for it. Sometimes I wish I was estranged from my kid."

"You have no idea what you're saying," Betsy says.

"I'm an idiot," Ben says. "I'm sorry. My mouth gets me in trouble."

"But you have amazing posture. And you might be a nice guy," Betsy says. "I thought you weren't, but I could have been wrong. My judgment isn't what it used to be."

Ben turns his head, and when he smiles at her, she recognizes the smile from earlier in the day. When she pulled herself out of the swimming pool, she thought the smile was menacing and maybe it is, but now she chooses to understand it otherwise.

"I used to be a dancer," he says. "That's why the posture. Not a bad gig for a straight boy."

"I can imagine," Betsy says.

"Mistake I made was marrying from the corps. And an American no less who couldn't wait to get back to California. I should have held out for a principal. I mean if she was going to leave first chance anyway. Then our idiot son decides to get married when he gets some girl pregnant, and they live in the Presidential Suite, but then they get an apartment and the next thing I know something's gone wrong and there's no more baby or maybe there never was a baby, and next thing I know he's staying in the apartment. And now I'm stuck with that one."

"It's a lot to take in," Betsy says, feeling herself swallowing as if she's actually consuming this information along with the hamburger smell filling the car.

"I bet you're something in bed," this man says. "Ever since I saw you in the pool, that's all I've been thinking about."

Betsy is not speechless, but she chooses not to respond. *I can't remember*, she thinks about saying. *Maybe I am.*

Crystal is making her way back to the car, looking down at the phone in the palm of her hand while she walks. When she looks up to get in, Betsy thinks Crystal might be holding back tears. She wants to say something comforting, but now she actually is speechless.

"Thanks, Pop!" a boy shouts out of an open window.

Ben waves, but it's a wave of dismissal, not a greeting.

Betsy doesn't know much, but she knows that. She doesn't know where her daughter is, she doesn't know when she's going to tell her mother to cancel the anniversary party, and she doesn't know when she'll ever feel that instead of supporting her, the earth is causing her knees to buckle and her body to fall into it.

Betsy does know she will wheel the suitcase she left in the motel lobby and follow this man with a dancer's posture and an Australian accent and all the wrong words into one of the many unoccupied rooms at his failing motel when they get back. She knows that when he pulls back the surprisingly delicate bedspread, the one nice feature in the otherwise unremarkable room with its plastic night tables and rolling desk chair, she will lock the deadbolt not to keep him out but to keep him in. She understands that her marriage has been over so long that this does not even qualify as a betrayal.

"Sometimes I just fucking hate him," Crystal says.

And now Betsy can see she is crying. This is what her daughter said about the boy at school who hurt her. *I fucking hate him.*

No, you don't, Betsy had said. *Hate's a strong word. You'll get over this.*

What do you know? Charlotte said. *Why can't you just be supportive?*

"I'm sorry," Betsy says now. "I hate him, too."

"Hey," Ben says. "That's my son."

Betsy shrugs. She can't tell if he's pretend-annoyed or not, and she realizes she doesn't really care. Tomorrow she will leave this motel and never see this man or his daughter-in-law again.

"Is this okay?" Ben says, turning around to face Betsy again as Crystal drives. He has rolled down his window, and Betsy nods.

She knows he will soon ask this same question in bed, his hands moving over her.

Is this okay? How about this? and she will nod, willing herself to inhabit a space outside of her own unfamiliar body.

But, for now, she shuts her eyes and listens, Ben's fingers tapping a staccato rhythm on the roof of a car in which she somehow finds herself a passenger.

Afterword

I want to thank all of my friends and family who have supported me with long conversations during walks, in person and on the phone. You all know who you are and how much I value you. I am grateful for my Pod, who made the pandemic less lonely and continue to make my life richer. Thank you to my amazing children, and to my mother, Joyce Greenberg Lott, for raising me in a house where books mattered.

A special thank you to Gina Caruso, my oldest friend and a relentless champion of my work. Thank you to Erica Lansdown for making me want to show up and write; Ginger Coriell, who manages to make an ocean between us feel like a few blocks; Sarah Michaelson, expert listener and inspiration; Lisa Wolff for her editing acumen; and Lisa Glatt, always. And thank you to my husband, Steve Perrin, for his critical eye, open heart and endless patience.

Finally, I want to thank Arroyo Seco Press for believing in these stories. I am eternally grateful for LeAnne's kindness and expert editing skills and for Tommy's care and vision.

Acknowledgements

The following stories have first appeared, sometimes in slightly different formats, in the following publications:

"Under the Radar," *LA Fiction Anthology,* Red Hen Press, May 2016

"How It Happens," *Mississippi Review* 50th Anniversary edition, Winter 2022

"Missing," *Santa Monica Review* 29.2, Fall 2017

"Remodel," *Cimarron Review* 174, Spring 2011

"Night Shift," *West Branch* 54, Spring 2004

"Viola," *West Branch Wired,* Summer 2011

"Come See Us Again," *Santa Monica Review* 31.1, Spring 2019

"Offering," *Silver Screen Reflections: An Anthology of Movie-Related Fiction, Poetry, and Essays,* Arroyo Seco Press, Fall 2023

"Shopping for Dad," *Pearl* 36, 2006

"Juggling,"*Washington Review* 8.5, February/March 1988

"Freshman," *Chiron Review* 83, 2008

"How This Works," *Aquifer: Florida Review Online,* November 2, 2020

"Illegal Baker," *Mochila Review* 3, 2002

"Stampede," *LitRag* 7, 1999

Biography

Suzanne Greenberg's novel *Lesson Plans* was a Library Journal Editor's Pick, and her short story collection *Speed-Walk and Other Stories* won a Drue Heinz Literature Prize. Her short fiction and creative nonfiction have appeared in numerous journals, including *Mississippi Review*, *Santa Monica Review*, *The Florida Review* and the *Washington Post Magazine*. She's the coauthor with Michael C. Smith of *Everyday Creative Writing: Panning for Gold in the Kitchen Sink* and, with Lisa Glatt, of two novels for children, *Abigail Iris: The One and Only* and *Abigail Iris: The Pet Project*. She received her BA from Hampshire College and her MFA from the University of Maryland. She teaches creative writing at California State University, Long Beach, where she's a professor of English.

www.suzannegreenberg.com @suzanne.a.greenberg

I know when I'm in a Suzanne Greenberg short story from the perfect way it unfolds and from the charm and flaws of her characters. *Shopping for Dad* is an impressive collection, full of tension, heart, and wit. Here, as in her award-winning *Speed-Walk*, I recognize Suzanne's voice—her quiet boldness, her profundity and precision, and the jolt of surprise as her characters reveal their private truths.

—Lisa Glatt, author of the novels *A Girl Becomes a Comma Like That* and *The Nakeds* and the short story collection, *The Apple's Bruise*

Suzanne Greenberg's stories, like those of Raymond Carver and Maile Meloy, are almost magically capable of elevating the lives of everyday individuals into realms of quiet—and often devastating—myth. Whether it's the soon-to-be-divorced woman in "Remodel" or the melancholic middle-aged sisters in "Offering," these are characters who inspire our empathy, our frustration, and our love while expertly capturing what it's like to live in the early decades of 21st Century America.

—Kareem Tayyar, author of *Keats in San Francisco & Other Poems*

Missing children, estranged spouses, and disappeared domestic objects call attention not only to loss and despair but also somehow to deadpan struggle and sardonic hope. Suzanne Greenberg's characters seem mostly to fail at living their individual lives but, weirdly, help each other, not diminished or lost, to collectively celebrate both the inexplicable yet logical desire for love and meaning. These stories are stubbornly honest, painful, and funny and hit, yes, very close to home.

—Andrew Tonkovich, editor of *Santa Monica Review*, founding editor of *Citric Acid: An Online Orange County Literary Arts Quarterly*, and host of *Bibliocracy Radio* on KPFK 90.7 FM